20

SPECIAL MESSAGE TO READERS

THE ULVERSCROFT FOUNDATION

(registered UK charity number 264873)

was established in 1972 to provide funds for research, diagnosis and treatment of eye diseases. Examples of major projects funded by the Ulverscroft Foundation are:

- The Children's Eye Unit at Moorfields Eye Hospital, London
- The Ulverscroft Children's Eye Unit at Great Ormond Street Hospital for Sick Children
- Funding research into eye diseases and treatment at the Department of Ophthalmology, University of Leicester
- The Ulverscroft Vision Research Group, Institute of Child Health
- Twin operating theatres at the Western Ophthalmic Hospital, London
- The Chair of Ophthalmology at the Royal Australian College of Ophthalmologists

You can help further the work of the Foundation by making a donation or leaving a legacy. Every contribution is gratefully received. If you would like to help support the Foundation or require further information, please contact:

THE ULVERSCROFT FOUNDATION
The Green, Bradgate Road, Anstey
Leicester LE7 7FU, England
Tel: (0116) 236 4325
website: www.ulverscroft-foundation.org.uk

MRS. BROWN AND THE CHRISTMAS GIFT

Caroline Brown once made a choice she deeply regrets, costing her the trust of a dear friend. Now she is determined to build a new life as the owner of a dressmaking shop in Chatternwell.

William Jackson has kept to himself ever since returning home from war. The spirited dressmaker down the street is a distraction he does not need — until an injury on Christmas Eve leaves him in her care. Her kindness and quiet strength unsettle him in ways he never expected.

Can the spirit of Christmas bring healing, hope, and the courage to open their hearts?

C. N. JARRETT

MRS. BROWN AND THE CHRISTMAS GIFT

Complete and Unabridged

LINFORD
Leicester

First published in Great Britain in 2023 as
Caroline Saves the Blacksmith

First Linford Edition
published 2025
by arrangement with
the author

A catalogue record for this book is available from the British Library.

ISBN 978–1–4448–5656–9

Published by
Ulverscroft Limited
Anstey, Leicestershire

Printed and bound by CPI Group (UK) Ltd.,
Croydon, CR0 4YY
This book is printed on acid-free paper

MIX
Paper | Supporting responsible forestry
FSC® C013604

Thank you to the tradespeople of Colonial Williamsburg for bringing history to life and answering my questions about trades in the 1700s with patience and expertise.

And, on the topic of history, I would like to thank my wonderful editor, Katie Jackson, whose keen eye is always on the lookout for anachronisms. She has not only helped me craft better stories, but helped me to ensure that they were true to the era.

Prologue:
The Beginning

Early Autumn, 1818

Tears streamed down Caroline Brown's cheeks as she packed her valise and a small trunk provided by Mrs. Harris.

She was leaving Baydon Hall, the only true home she had ever known, for a new position in the local doctor's household that Mrs. Harris had arranged for her. Yet she did not deserve the post.

I deserve to be turned out of the manor, without any assistance, for what I have done.

Regret and shame warred in her chest, which felt too small and tight to contain the emotions threatening to brim over.

It is all my fault.

She had lost her home, her friends, and her self-respect, and for what? For a few stolen kisses in a nobleman's arms. So desperate for attention, she had succumbed to temptation and betrayed a dear friend.

Three days earlier, Miss Annabel Ridley, the daughter of the baron at Baydon Hall, had caught her in an embrace with the lady's betrothed, the Earl of Saunton, in the stables. Lord Saunton had failed to defend her, and the young miss had been justifiably enraged, unwilling to see or speak to Caroline. Nevertheless, Miss Annabel had seen fit to provide her with a reference for her position as a maid and bade Mrs. Harris, the housekeeper, find her employment elsewhere.

It was very generous, given the circumstances, but Miss Annabel had always been kind. As a girl, Miss Annabel had taught Caroline to read and bestowed gifts of fabric, ribbons, and thread on her birthday each year to encourage her interest in sewing. Now, despite the horrendous deceit, Miss Annabel had assisted Caroline with her future position.

But the young mistress of Baydon Hall was furious and distraught. She had instructed that Caroline remain out of sight in the kitchens and leave the estate as quickly as possible.

The unexpected generosity added to Caroline's crushing guilt. She wished she could plead for forgiveness, to assure Miss Annabel that she had seen the error of her ways and wished to make amends for betraying their friendship, which had meant so much to her. But she had no amends to offer.

I am a dishonourable woman.

Worse, she was a disloyal friend, undeserving of the help she was receiving. Her grandmother would turn in her grave to hear how Caroline had thrown away the opportunity afforded her by the old woman's friendship with Mrs. Harris. One of her last acts before dying had been to write to the housekeeper to request her help with the then-thirteen-year-old Caroline, who was about to lose her last living relation. Mrs. Harris had offered employment as a favour to her old friend, and Caroline had been summoned into service at Baydon Hall.

Since Grandmama had died, the servants, along with Miss Annabel, were Caroline's only family. She had let all of them down, and in doing so, had ruined Miss Annabel's happiness.

A few tender words from a handsome nobleman, and compliments to her figure, and Caroline had allowed herself to be lured into a series of impassioned kisses with a rogue. Fresh sobs tore through her chest, despair a physical pain. How would she ever forgive herself for what she had done?

1
The Meeting

8 November, 1820

Caroline waved goodbye to Mr. and Mrs. Thompson and their daughter and gently shut the door of her shop, *Mrs. Brown's Elegant Millinery & Dress-Rooms*, to draw an exhilarated breath. The scent of wood, fabric, and beeswax invaded her senses, and she gave a deep sigh of happiness.

The shop was now hers and hers alone. As of today, she was officially a modiste — the proprietress of her own business. Well . . . hers except for the interest-free loan from Lord Saunton that she must repay as profits allowed.

Caroline still experienced moments of unreality, wondering if she had dreamt all that had happened in the past few months. Lord Saunton had summoned her to London, nearly two years after the incident in the stables, to apologise for the disruption he had caused to her life. He had offered her financial assistance, but instead of accepting charity, Caroline had seized the opportunity to request the loan Miss Annabel had once intended to provide following her planned marriage to Lord Saunton.

Of course, Miss Annabel never married Lord Saunton. Caroline had since learned from local gossip in Filminster that Miss Annabel had married the Duke of Halmesbury and now lived somewhere nearby in Wiltshire.

Lord Saunton had corrected his wayward behaviour and wed a young woman in London, for which Caroline could only be grateful. His offer to help her pursue her dream of opening a shop had been part of his effort to make amends. He had set his man, Mr. Johnson, to find a suitable location and assist her in preparing for a successful enterprise.

The humiliating events that led to her proprietorship must remain a secret now that she had begun afresh in Wiltshire. It would ruin her business before it began if the townspeople learnt she had been compromised — or if they assumed she was a kept woman.

That will not happen.

Those who knew the truth of her past were the Duke and Duchess of Halmesbury, the Baron of Filminster, Mrs. Harris, Lord and Lady Saunton, along with his men, Johnson and Long, and Caroline herself. Thus far, all involved had been discreet, and Caroline was the only one living in Chatternwell. She supposed Mr. Thompson, the earl's half-brother, might be aware, but he had given no sign.

As long as Caroline focused on her business and formed no personal entanglements, she could safeguard her secret. She had employed the same caution in Filminster while working for the local doctor.

For months after being caught in the stables, Caroline had lived in fear that her shame would be exposed. But then, thanks to her book learning and knowledge of numbers — skills Miss Annabel had imparted to prepare her for business — she had earned a promotion to housekeeper. That had been the day she realised her secret was safe. No one intended to reveal that she had once been caught kissing her mistress's betrothed.

She had vowed to devote herself to her duties and avoid forming close attachments, and she had thrived in that role. If she adhered to the same rule here, she would succeed again. Caroline had been in Chatternwell for two months preparing for today's opening, and she was satisfied with the progress she had made.

Lord Saunton and his brother, Mr. Barclay Thompson, a renowned architect, had made a point of endorsing her shop. Lord Saunton had ordered a banyan for himself — loudly enough for other patrons to hear — and Mr. Thompson's wife and daughter had each placed orders for carriage dresses.

Word that an earl had visited a modiste's shop spread swiftly. Caroline had gained introductions to other merchants and secured several high-priced commissions once the local elite arrived to see the mysterious modiste with such noble patrons.

When Lord Saunton first announced his intention to attend her opening, Caroline had worried her reputation might suffer. Would the townsfolk guess the truth of their history? But he had ensured propriety, attending with family members and making it known that he was visiting his nearby estate. Loud, artful remarks about his surprise at finding such an elegant shop in town were made within earshot of affluent customers, and Caroline appreciated his tact.

Still, it felt like a dream. She was truly running her own shop. The gloves and scarves displayed in the window, the bolts of fine fabrics fitted into cubbyholes soaring up the walls — all of it was hers.

She ran her hand along the smooth walnut counter and hummed quietly. After what she had done to Miss Annabel, she would never have dared to hope for this future. Yet when the opportunity came, she had taken it, knowing it was her last chance to claim the life she had once imagined.

Here in Chatternwell, she was respected. The dishonour of her past — a few impulsive kisses shared with the wrong man — was a private memory, one she kept close as a warning. Never again would she risk forming an attachment that might destroy everything she had built.

Work, and only work, was the path to redemption.

A smile touched her lips as she caught sight of a little girl pressing her nose to the shop window. The child came by often, mesmerised by the ribbons, though she had yet to venture inside now that the shop was open. Her hair was a wild tangle of mousy brown, and Caroline longed to offer her a bit of ribbon to tame it.

Still humming, she tidied a stack of fashion plates and glanced back to the window.

But something was different. The girl's shoulders were slumped, and Caroline thought she saw tears glinting on her cheeks. She straightened, alarmed.

She did not know the child or her family, but someone cared for her — the girl's garments, though worn, were clean and carefully mended.

Biting her lip, Caroline reminded herself that she must build a friendly rapport in town, even if she could not allow herself deeper ties. She walked around the counter, paused a moment to gather her resolve, and then opened the shop door.

* * *

William Jackson stood at the mullioned window of the Chatternwell post office, waiting for the clerk to finish assisting Mrs. Butterworth. With a bored sigh, he watched little Annie Greer peering into the window of the new dress-rooms across the road.

He wondered how the Greers were faring. He really ought to have called on them more often. Brian Greer had served in the same regiment —William had not known the man well — but he had fallen the same day as William's cousin Charles, at the farmhouse they had defended against Boney's army.

William's only excuse was that, after decades of war with the French, every town in England was scattered with widows. Annie and her mother had simply slipped his mind.

A slight frown creased his brow when he noticed that Annie's small shoulders were shaking. Was the child crying?

He stepped forward to gain a clearer view, but his attention was swiftly diverted when the shop door opened and a woman stepped out. His breath caught at the sight of her — Annie Greer's plight momentarily forgotten. This must be the newly arrived mantua-maker, if the local gossips were to be believed, though none had mentioned how young or striking the proprietress was.

Her wheat-coloured hair was swept into an elegant coiffure that revealed a fair, oval face. A pointed chin lent her an air of delicate determination, while thick lashes framed eyes whose colour he could not yet discern. Her wide, full mouth was at once soft and resolute, and the deep mulberry of her gown offset her complexion to perfection.

It had been many years since William had allowed himself to feel anything. That part of him had been silenced on the battlefield at Waterloo, when battle rage had overtaken his senses. He had welcomed the numbness when he awoke in the field hospital. It had spared him the agony of losing Charles. And he had clung to it when he returned to Chatternwell five years ago to inform his uncle and aunt of their son's death — news that shattered them before his eyes.

From that day forth, William had lived by logic, keeping emotion at bay. He had stepped out of the role of nephew and taken on the mantle of son, assuming his cousin's place as his penance for convincing Charles to join him in the army.

But that belonged to the past, a door he had closed long ago.

Now, in the present, he watched as

the young woman gently beckoned Annie Greer inside. For the first time in years, a strange sensation stirred in his chest — rising up into his throat and settling in his mouth — as if his heart had stirred and taken a solitary beat.

As the pair disappeared into the interior of *Mrs. Brown's Elegant Millinery & Dress-Rooms*, William exhaled slowly. The truth was plain. If he meant to preserve his peace of mind, he would do well to keep well away from that shop.

* * *

Caroline ushered the weeping girl into the back room. As they passed through the doorway, she swept aside the curtain, allowing a clear view of the front of the shop.

Mrs. Jones looked up from the worktable where she and her eldest daughter, Mary Beth, were sewing gowns. The seamstress's round face creased into a welcoming smile. 'Mrs. Brown, there be fresh tea in the pot.'

She gestured towards the hearth with her needle still in hand. Both women were positioned near the window where the light was strongest — every seamstress's greatest ally.

Caroline had enticed the town's most talented needlewomen with fair wages and regular hours. Many worked from home, but Mrs. Jones and Mary Beth preferred the quiet of the back room. They claimed the light was better, but Caroline suspected it also allowed them a bit of peace from their bustling household — and a quiet cup of tea.

She nodded, guiding the little girl to a workbench near the door, then moved towards the teapot. Her grandmother had always said that few troubles in life could not be eased by a good cup of tea. Whatever had brought the child to tears would be more easily imparted with something warm in her hands.

The seamstresses cast curious glances at the sniffling child but soon returned to their sewing. Mary Beth resumed a tale about a fight that had broken out at the tavern the previous night.

Caroline poured two cups of tea. She added a dash of milk to her own, but no sugar — experience had taught her that too much sweet made her sluggish, and she had no time for fatigue.

To the second cup, she added generous milk and an extra spoonful of sugar. If the girl was anything like Caroline had been at her age, she would prefer it sweet and mild. And according to the doctor she had worked for, sugar was a remedy for shock.

Caroline placed the cups on the table and sat across from her.

'What is your name, little one?'

'Annie,' came the hoarse reply. 'Annie Greer.'

The child's tears had ceased, but her expression remained bleak, her reddened eyes fixed on the cup before her. Caroline's heart twisted at the sight.

No personal relationships, do you hear?

She silenced the voice. Now was not the time.

'And why are you so upset, Annie

Greer?'

The girl was too thin, with pale skin and the hollow look of a child who did not eat enough. Her gown had been let out and mended multiple times.

'My mum is sending me away to Bath, and I don't want to go.'

Caroline tapped the teacup gently to encourage her to drink. Annie obeyed, taking a cautious sip. The taste seemed to soothe her, and she drank with greater enthusiasm. When she set the cup down, only half remained, and her features had softened.

'What is in Bath?'

'My mum found someone who would take me on, but I cannot leave her alone. Mum is ill, and she needs me.'

'There is no one else to help care for her?'

'No. It is just the two of us. She tried to find me a place here in Chatternwell, but no one is hiring.'

Caroline mulled this over as she sipped her tea. She had not yet taken on any apprentices, as she was still lodging nearby and had no household of her own. Apprenticeship often required room and board — something she could not yet provide.

And you are not to get entangled with the townsfolk.

'What sort of position in Bath?'

The girl's throat worked as she choked out the word. 'Washerwoman.'

Caroline winced. It was a grim path for a child. Exhausting, and with little hope of advancement. Clearly, Mrs. Greer was desperate.

Do not do it, Caroline. You swore you would not get involved again.

But she could not look into Annie's face and ignore what she had once been herself: a girl alone with an ailing guardian, frightened and uncertain of the future.

Her own fortune had changed when Mrs. Harris, honouring an old friendship with Caroline's grandmother, had promised to find her a position. Then Miss Annabel, observing Caroline's skill with a needle, had arranged for her to be apprenticed in the arts of millinery and mantua-making.

Without that act of kindness, she would not now be mistress of her own shop.

'Would you like to learn to sew?'

Annie looked up. Her face was still damp with tears. Caroline took out a handkerchief and gently dabbed her cheeks.

'I can sew.' Annie tugged at the sleeve of her dress to show a neat little darn near the seam.

'That is excellent work.'

'Thank you.'

Caroline drew in a breath. She was about to break her vow. But what was the point of success if it could not be used to lift someone else?

'How about I take you on as an apprentice?'

Annie lit up — then immediately sagged. 'I cannot. I must go home each night to care for Mum. And we have no money now that she cannot work much. I need a position that pays.'

'I believe we can manage something. I do not yet have room and board to offer, so I would pay you the value of that instead. You may return home to your mother each evening.'

Annie's eyes widened. 'Truly? I can work here and still stay with Mum?'

There were risks. If Mrs. Greer's health failed, Caroline might find herself with a young charge to care for.

Are you truly prepared for that? This could grow complicated.

Caroline squared her shoulders. Just this once, she would make an exception. Because once, someone had made an exception for her.

'You may begin tomorrow, if your mum agrees. Tell her to come see me in the morning. If we reach an understanding, I shall have a contract drawn up for her to sign.'

Annie clapped her hands, eyes shining.

Caroline smiled and gestured at the cup. 'Finish your tea, Annie.'

The child did so cheerfully. When they had finished, Caroline led her to the window display.

'As a seamstress and a member of my staff, it is important to tie your hair back so that you may see your work. Which ribbon would you like?'

Annie's jaw dropped. 'A ribbon? Of my own?'

'Pick one.'

The girl examined the spools intently, her fingers alighting on a length of scarlet. 'May I have this one?'

'You may.'

Caroline reached into the drawer for her scissors, measured and cut the ribbon, then gently gathered the girl's hair. She plaited it and tied it off with the ribbon, drawing it forward so Annie could see the bow.

'Cor! It is beautiful!'

Caroline smiled. 'You will learn to make many beautiful things here.'

Annie left shortly afterwards, having agreed on a time for her mother's visit. Despite her misgivings, Caroline felt in her heart that she had done the right thing.

* * *

William had purchased provisions and was returning to his cottage with parcels under his arm, enjoying a rare respite from his work.

The walk should have taken only a few minutes, but somehow he found himself hesitating outside the mantua-maker's shop. It was devilishly tempting to enter under some pretext, if only to see her again. Perhaps confirm the colour of her eyes or admire the curve of her mouth.

He quashed the thought.

As if summoned, Annie Greer emerged from the shop, a broad smile lighting her face. William felt a brief jolt of surprise — had he misread her sorrow earlier? She looked quite smart, her hair neatly plaited with a scarlet ribbon.

'Enjoying your day, Annie?'

She beamed, nodding enthusiastically. 'It is a marvellous day, Mr. Jackson! I am to be a seamstress!' she proclaimed, then skipped off down the street in a flutter of skirts.

William stared after her in surprise. Had the new shopkeeper hired Annie? That would certainly be good news for Mrs. Greer. He had only just heard, while about town, that the poor woman was unwell.

Everywhere he had gone that day, the women of Chatternwell had spoken with admiration of the new dressmaker and her elegant shop. If Mrs. Brown had indeed offered Annie employment, it was commendable — something William might have done himself had he known of their need.

He ought to return home. He had no business lingering. Annie was clearly well. Yet he found himself still standing at the door.

Go home, William.

But something about the shop — the woman within — held him in place.

This is absurd. Leave it be.

He took a steadying breath and turned towards the smithy.

* * *

It was late afternoon, almost closing time, when the shop door opened and closed with the gentle tinkle of the bell. Caroline was mid-way through counting spools of thread, her pencil moving swiftly across the page as she jotted a number down in her notebook. She turned with a welcoming smile, prepared to greet the late-day visitor.

To her surprise, one of the blacksmiths from down the street stood just inside the doorway. She had never seen him up close before. He was usually a distant figure standing in front of the smithy. Now, standing in the soft light of her shop, he seemed even larger, his shoulders broad enough to fill the frame of the doorway. His presence commanded the room, and she found herself straightening instinctively.

Caroline had not been aware of how solidly built the man was, with thick shoulders and a height that easily surpassed six feet. The parcels tucked under his arm looked almost comically small compared to the breadth of his chest and the sturdy lines of his arms, clearly accustomed to hard work. His dark hair was cropped neatly, his beard trimmed close to his jaw, giving him an air of rugged respectability. His eyes — strikingly blue — were sharp and observant, the sort that seemed to take in everything with quiet assessment. For the briefest of moments, she had the oddest sensation that those eyes were searching her soul, though she brushed off the thought as fanciful nonsense.

She had sworn off all men after the events at Baydon Hall, vowing to keep her heart and her ambitions firmly under her own control. But standing so close to someone so unmistakably capable, she found it unexpectedly difficult to recall the reasons for her vow. He seemed to radiate confidence and strength — traits she had learnt to mistrust, but here they were accompanied by a quiet stillness that unsettled her far more than she liked to admit. Caroline's hands smoothed over her skirts as she tried to maintain her composure, aware of the odd flutter that had taken up residence in her chest.

The man was scrupulously clean, dressed in sturdy buckskins, well-made black boots, a crisp linen shirt, and a waistcoat that fit him well. His clothing, though simple, was well-tailored and spoke of a man who valued neatness despite his laborious work. But his expression was severe, his square jaw set with determination. He was not the sort given to idle chatter or unnecessary smiles; she imagined him to be direct and to the point, with little patience for frivolities.

'So, you are the new mantua-maker?' he asked, his voice steady and unhurried. As a greeting, it was rather abrupt, but there was no malice in it — just simple curiosity.

Caroline resisted the urge to bristle. Men of trade often did not understand the subtleties of women's fashion, and she would not fault him for it. After all, she knew little of the art of shaping metal or what it took to bend iron to one's will. Fair was fair.

As she arrived at this conclusion, Caroline gave herself a brief nod to acknowledge that she had the right of it, before beaming widely.

'There are three mantua-makers in Chatternwell. I, however, am a milliner and a modiste,' she corrected him gently, her tone light and pleasant.

'What is the difference?'

Caroline nearly frowned at his curtness but caught herself. 'I am certain the mantua-makers are highly competent and an integral part of the community, but the title of modiste implies a certain freshness of fashion sense — someone knowledgeable about the latest trends. There are ladies in town who possess a particular refinement of taste and elegance and require a modiste to handle their wardrobe needs.'

'Aha. It allows you to sell the more expensive fabric.'

'Well . . . yes . . . but . . . with greater profits, I am able to share my success with the seamstresses I employ. I pay higher wages and offer better hours.'

'Are you not afraid you are taking the livelihood from the other mantua-makers?'

Caroline smiled broadly. This was a question she could answer with confidence. 'Not at all. We discovered that the more elegant ladies who are in need of a modiste have been forced to travel to Bath or London for their gowns. Now they have access to the latest London designs right here, in the comfort of their own town. Many households cannot afford our services, so the trade of the other shops remains undisturbed.'

'We?'

She hesitated, not sure how to respond. Why had she allowed that to slip? 'My business adviser, Mr. Johnson. He works for my primary investor.'

If the blacksmith asked another prying question — such as who her primary investor was — she would be forced to redirect the conversation. She would never reveal her connection to the Earl of Saunton lest the townsfolk — she suppressed a wince — drew the mostly correct conclusion.

She could not deny the flicker of irritation that coursed through her veins at the gentleman's interrogation. To her dismay, it was accompanied by a curious sense of awareness that unsettled her. The blacksmith was gruff, but undeniably handsome and sharp-witted, his questions showing a mind that grasped more than she would have expected. It quickened her pulse slightly, leaving her scrambling to maintain her composure. It was a combination of frustration and unexpected interest.

She straightened her shoulders and shook off the thoughts. It would not do.

Caroline! You vowed there would be no men! Stop admiring the brute and get him out of your shop!

The blacksmith nodded. 'And how does one become a modiste? You were apprenticed?'

'I was. Signora Ricci serves the nobility in London and graciously taught me the details of running a fashionable dressmaker's shop.'

'The details of running a shop . . . Did you serve an apprenticeship in millinery and dressmaking somewhere else, then?'

Caroline nearly grimaced. This man was far too clever. He had caught every slip, proving she would need to prepare a better story for just such a situation if she did not wish to reveal too many details of her past. Pinning her smile in place, she gave him his answer.

'I was in service at Baydon Hall in Somerset. The housekeeper, Mrs. Harris, apprenticed me in the sewing arts.'

The blacksmith frowned, tilting his head in question. 'Is there much call for a seamstress in a stately home?'

'There is a surprising number of tasks. Repairs to curtains and cushions. Mending livery, mobcaps, and other household attire. In theory, I worked in the kitchen, but I mostly did needlework for my entire tenure under Mrs. Harris, who had vast experience in such things.'

He drew a heavy breath. 'Modiste.'

It sounded as if the blacksmith were trying the word out, feeling the shape of it on his tongue. Caroline's eyes widened slightly at the way he spoke it, his tone careful and deliberate. She found herself studying the way his mouth moved around the syllables and then immediately scolded herself for the foolishness of it. *That aspect of your life is dead and buried!* she reminded herself firmly.

'I am William Jackson.'

Caroline stepped back in surprise.

The man was not just a blacksmith. He was the blacksmith, owner of the largest smithy in Chatternwell with numerous journeymen and apprentices in his employ. From what she had heard, he was an astute tradesman who stocked an array of iron and steel tools, locks, and other mechanisms for purchase. Considering his accomplishments, he was rather humbly attired. Caroline supposed he might be in want of a wife to coax him into displaying his success.

She had gathered from her staff's gossip that the smithy itself rivalled the best in Bath for its excellent work. Apparently, the man had set quite a few female hearts aflutter, but had shown no sign of interest. It was surprising to meet him and discover firsthand his lack of social finesse. It must have been his appearance and business acumen that had the women of Chatternwell so enthralled, not his fine manners.

'I need a gift for my neighbour, Mrs. Heeley. Something suitable for an elderly woman who does not get around much.'

Now that she was no longer being interrogated, Caroline found herself oddly charmed by the gruff tones of his deep voice. Mr. Jackson had a presence that was impossible to ignore, his steady manner almost reassuring. She was unused to such towering strength paired with such quietness, and it made her acutely aware of the difference in their statures. *Goodness, he is rather compelling*, she thought, catching herself before she stared too long.

'Of course. How about a lovely shawl to keep her warm in the winter months? We have just received a fine selection.' Caroline was proud of how even her voice sounded, even if it had taken a fraction too long to respond.

Mr. Jackson raised his broad shoulders in a shrug. He was a man of few words. Caroline smiled encouragingly and steered him towards the shawls, her hands brushing over the soft wool and cashmere with practised ease.

Fifteen minutes later, his purchase made, it was almost a relief to watch him exit the shop. His presence had a way of filling the room, and she found herself letting out a breath she had not realised she was holding. There was a quiet strength about him, one that made the small space feel warmer, more substantial. And yet, she knew she would need to be careful. She must be a chaste woman after the painful lessons of her past. Nay, she would need to keep her distance from Mr. Jackson with his rugged handsomeness and steady gaze. She had a reputation to uphold in her adopted home, and she would not risk it for a passing fancy.

It had been easier when she was in

service. Not only was there no time for relationships, but one was not permitted to marry, which had made her vow much simpler to keep.

The blacksmith was undeniably intriguing despite his gruff manner, and Caroline vowed to stay at her end of the street and leave Mr. Jackson to his.

2
The Request

Christmas Eve, 1820

Annie finished fastening the last Christmas bough to the shop window. Turning around, she planted her small fists on her hips and declared, 'There you are, Mrs. Brown! All dressed up for the holidays!'

Caroline clapped her hands and smiled in acknowledgement. She did not observe the holidays herself, but she had commissioned Mrs. Greer to prepare the boughs and sprigs for the shop as an excuse to offer her some coin. She could not deny the pleasure of the greenery's fresh scent, which she would enjoy until Twelfth Night, when custom demanded it be taken down to avoid ill fortune.

Annie had filled out in the past weeks, and Mrs. Greer's health was gradually improving, which made it all worthwhile. The child had proved a diligent worker — sweeping the shop, waxing the counters, and dusting the shelves with energy. She had even begun assisting with simple sewing, and Caroline had sent small projects home for Mrs. Greer to complete at her leisure.

Caroline suspected the widow's ailments had stemmed, at least in part, from poor diet and worry. Now, with steady income and nourishing food, both mother and daughter were showing signs of recovery. Caroline might not be celebrating the holidays herself, but she was ensuring the Greers had the means to.

'Well done, Annie! It is very festive. Tell your mother she did a splendid job.'

'It smells so lovely!' Annie took a deep breath, clearly delighted by the scent of rosemary woven into the boughs, along with holly, ivy, and Christmas rose, as she had enthusiastically recited that morning.

Caroline grinned, taking an exaggerated sniff for Annie's benefit. It smelled like a forest — clean and sharp and green.

'You have done excellent work, young lady. You should go assist your mother in preparing your Christmas feast for tomorrow.'

Annie's smile dimmed. 'Are you sure you will not come, Mrs. Brown?'

'Do not worry about me. I have work to complete. I plan to finish my walking dress over the next few days. When you return on Tuesday, I shall be able to show it to you.'

She had allowed herself to grow closer to the Greers than she had intended. Spending the holiday with them would only deepen that connection, and she could not afford further attachment.

'Now, come see your board for the week.'

She had been sending a basket of food home with Annie each week. Eggs and fresh vegetables to assist the girl and her mother with their health. She called it Annie's keep because the girl not living with her was not customary for apprentices. Truthfully, the wages she paid were meant to be in lieu of the room and board she would have provided if she had had a home. Referring to the basket of food that Caroline purchased from the market each week as keep was an excuse to discreetly take care of the Greers while preserving their pride. It did not cost her much, and she had minimal personal expenses to worry about, but it clearly made a difference for them.

She reached beneath the counter and brought out the large hamper, placing it on the counter. 'Have a look inside.'

Annie approached with curiosity, then lifted the chequered cloth. Her eyes widened.

'Is that — ?'

'I included mince pies and oranges this week,' Caroline said gently. 'And I placed an order with Mr. Andrews that you may collect after service tomorrow.'

Annie blinked. 'Mr. Andrews? Which one?'

'The baker.'

The girl's eyes shone. 'Never say, Mrs. Brown! Is it a Christmas goose?'

Caroline nodded, warmed by the child's joy. 'For you and your mother. A proper feast.'

Annie's lip trembled. Then she darted around the counter and threw her arms around Caroline's waist. 'Please come eat with us, Mrs. Brown. It is not right for you to be alone on Christmas.'

Caroline's heart gave a dull ache. It would be her first Christmastide truly alone. As a girl, she had spent the holiday with her grandmother. After Grandmama's death, she had observed the day with the servants at Baydon Hall, and more recently, with the doctor's household in Filminster.

But she had drawn too near the Greers already. She needed to remain apart, to protect her secret. She had no right to such closeness — not after what she had done.

No need to think of that. Work will keep the memories at bay.

'Christmas is for family, Annie. You should be with your mother.'

A soft sniffle came from where the

girl's face pressed to her. 'You are family, Mrs. Brown.'

Caroline smiled and hugged her, then gently set her away. 'Go enjoy your holiday. And do not forget the goose.'

Annie bobbed her head, struggling slightly with the weight of the basket. 'Thank you, Mrs. Brown. Merry Christmas!'

Caroline waved as the child departed, then returned to her account books. The shop was quiet — being Sunday, Mrs. Jones and Mary Beth were home preparing their own Christmas feast.

As Caroline scratched numbers with her graphite pencil, a heavy silence settled over the room. The streets, lively earlier, had gone still. Most shops were closed for the Sabbath. She might be the only merchant at work. Finishing her accounts, she slipped the books beneath the counter and looked about. The stillness was eerie. She decided it was time to turn her attention to the walking dress before memory and melancholy crept in.

In the back, she approached the gown

hanging in the corner. On the day she learnt she would own her shop, she had purchased a fine bolt of Prussian blue velvet using her savings. She had resolved to create a signature garment — a walking dress that would showcase her craftsmanship and symbolise her new beginning.

She had sewn it piece by piece in her spare hours. The shoulders were stitched with textured loops and whorls. The high collar folded over gracefully, its edge embroidered with ornate detail. The hem was scalloped, and the trimming spanned two inches of intricate work. The bodice and cuffs remained unfinished.

When complete, it would be the finest garment she had ever made. A testament to everything she had achieved. But no dress, no matter how finely sewn, could fill the hollow place within her.

You threw away your chance for family when you betrayed Miss Annabel.

Caroline shook her head and reached for the gown. If she could not have kinship, she would at least have purpose. And purpose, she reminded herself, had always brought her comfort.

* * *

William closed up the smithy and made his way towards the cottages at the end of Market Street.

He had given his journeymen and apprentices time off for the holiday, and the forge would remain closed until Tuesday, the day after Christmas, save for urgent repairs. He had left a note on the smithy door that he could be found at his cottage, though he expected no business. The townsfolk were swept up in festive cheer.

He had plans of his own.

The widow next door, Mrs. Heeley, had departed the previous day to visit her daughter in Bath. At last, he could tend to her roof — without her knowledge.

Proud and fiercely independent, Mrs. Heeley insisted on paying or bartering for every kindness offered. But William had noticed a leak in her roof during his last visit and resolved to repair it while she was away. The work would be done quietly, and she would be none the wiser.

He had purchased the slate tiles a week ago. Now, all he needed were his tools and the old ladder behind his cottage. Usually, one of his apprentices would assist with such work, but he had sent them home early to ensure they reached their families in time for the holiday.

The street was quiet save for laughter and music drifting from the inn near his house. William did not mind solitude, but the holidays always brought back memories of Charles.

They had been of an age — more like brothers than cousins. After the deaths of William's parents, he had come to live with Uncle Albert and Aunt Gertrude. Apprenticed in the smithy, he and Charles had run wild during Christmastide, drinking too much ale and daring too many girls to kiss them under the mistletoe.

But those days were gone. Charles

was gone. His parents had retired to Cornwall to grieve in peace, leaving the smithy in William's care.

Work had become his balm, his penance. And his purpose.

It was my fault. Charles would never have gone to war if not for me.

He could still hear himself stating such idiotic sentiments.

'It will be a lark! We shall spill French blood and protect the liberty of England!'

Foolish words, spoken by a boy who had not yet seen what musket fire could do. He and Charles had marched off in their red coats, full of dreams and courage.

Now only William remained.

He reached Mrs. Heeley's cottage and circled round the back, laying down the tiles and retrieving his tools. Then he unearthed the old ladder and leaned it against the honey-coloured stone.

He hoisted the bag of slate over his shoulder and began the climb. Halfway up, one of the rungs groaned beneath his weight. He noted the weakness — it would need reinforcing before the ladder was stored again.

But first, there was a roof to mend. He intended to finish the repairs today. If all went well, he might spend Christmas drawing the new lock design that had taken root in his mind. He would have time to test it, refine it. That was how he celebrated — with work.

The tiles came away easily. He tossed the old ones into the small garden below and fitted the new in their place.

As he paused, he sat back on his heels and stretched his shoulders. A light flurry of snow had begun to fall, silent and slow.

He looked out across the rooftops, their slate glistening under the gathering dusk. Chimneys sent up curls of smoke, and the sky had turned a brooding iron grey. To the west, the pale winter sun dipped low behind the hills.

He remembered another winter afternoon like this — many years past. He and Charles had been mending Uncle Albert's roof after a storm. They had sat, side by side, feet dangling, speaking of the future.

Charles had planned to marry the girl he had been courting. They would share the smithy, raise families, and one day, take over the business together. They had laughed about the mischief their sons would get into, as wild as they themselves had once been.

William closed his eyes against the memory. He had buried Charles with his own hands. He had carried him from the field at Waterloo.

Only work dulled the ache.

When he opened his eyes, the snowfall had thickened. It was time to go. He packed his tools into his valise and made his way to the ladder.

The snowflakes melted on contact with the still-warm slate, leaving the surface slick. Fortunately, the job was finished — were the weather to worsen, tomorrow's work would have been impossible.

He stepped carefully onto the ladder.

Halfway down, a sharp crack split the

air.

The rung beneath his foot gave way.

'Blazes!'

William fell. His boot caught in the collapsing ladder, and he crashed to the ground, landing hard on his back. The air rushed from his lungs as pain exploded through his body.

* * *

When Caroline looked up from her embroidery, she realised the light from the back window had faded. The sun was setting, and snow was falling, casting the room in a soft, grey hue. Her shop, nestled among other merchants, lay in utter stillness. Too still.

A quiet melancholy settled over her, as pervasive and chill as the dusk beyond the panes. She set aside the walking dress on the worktable and scolded herself silently.

It is the holidays. Cheer up, Caroline.

With resolve, she rose to her feet and began humming the verses she had once sung with her grandmother at this time of year. She checked the back door, secured the lock, and moved about the workroom, lighting each candle and lantern until the shadows receded. Drawing a breath, she lifted her voice in song to fill the hushed silence:

While shepherds watched their flocks
by night,
all seated on the ground,
an angel of the Lord came down,
and glory shone around.

She stepped into the front of the shop and lit it fully. As light flooded the room, so too did her spirits rise. She had much for which to be thankful. Her walking dress would soon be complete — an exquisite piece of fine workmanship. Her seamstresses were thriving, the shop's reputation growing. Mr. Johnson had just confirmed her business was on course, and Caroline could take pride in her success. Little Annie Greer was healthy and bright, and Mrs. Greer's strength was returning.

'Fear not,' said he, for mighty dread
had seized their troubled mind;
'glad tidings of great joy I bring
to you and all mankind.'

And she herself had stayed the course — no man had tempted her since Lord Saunton. She had held fast to her vow, maintaining the dignity she had once cast aside.

'To you, in David's town, this day
is born of David's line
a Savior, who is Christ the Lord;
and this shall be the sign:'

She might be alone this Christmas Eve, but she had a new life, built on integrity and hard work. And she could sing as loudly as she pleased in her empty, candlelit shop.

'The heavenly Babe you there shall find
to human view displayed,

all meanly wrapped in swathing bands,
and in a manger laid.'

She returned to the back room to prepare her tea. Whilst the kettle boiled, she found the biscuits she had purchased earlier from Mr. Andrews and arranged them on a small plate. She ought to return to her lodgings, but her landlady had left to visit family in Bath, and the thought of sitting in a quiet house, alone, was less appealing than remaining in her bright, warm shop.

Thus spoke the angel. Suddenly
appeared a shining throng
of angels praising God, who thus
addressed their joyful song:

The townsfolk here in Chatternwell had accepted her with open arms — that was another blessing she had not yet counted!

Raising her voice, she sang the last verse loudly as she set down her teacup. Her loneliness was a choice. A penance for her past mistakes. She had acquired many fine acquaintances here in the town, and her work was all she required.

'All glory be to God on high,
and to the earth be peace;
to those on whom his favor rests
goodwill shall never cease.'

Silence descended once more. Biting her lip, she tried to think of something else to sing. Opening her mouth, she —

A loud knocking resounded from the front door. Caroline's mouth clamped shut as she frowned in confusion.

Who on earth —

Another loud knocking.

Whoever it was, they were frantic to get her attention. The very windows rattled from the blows on the door.

Caroline briskly strode across the workroom to enter the front of the shop, more than a little nervous about whom she might find outside on Christmas Eve. Her fears were eased when she saw through the windows that it was

Dr. Hadley, one of the town's two doctors. He was a jovial sort and quite popular for his generous spirit.

Hurrying over, Caroline unlocked the door to let him in.

Dr. Hadley was a well-fed man of average height with salt-and-pepper hair. He had a broad face with a thick moustache and a vaguely Mediterranean look about him. Currently, he looked harried rather than his usual cheerful self.

'Is everything all right, Dr. Hadley?'

His gravelly voice revealed his anxiety. 'Mrs. Brown, I am so pleased to find you. I swear the entire street is deserted for the Eve celebrations. I could not find a single soul of any use!'

'Are you in need of assistance?'

The doctor swiped a white handkerchief over his forehead, mopping up the sweat of his exertions. 'I hate to impose, Mrs. Brown. There were people about when I was called to Mr. Jackson's, but by the time I was done treating him, I could find no one to help. John Bow is here to drive me urgently to his farm so

I can attend to his wife. She is in labour and needs me right away, but I must find someone to take care of Mr. Jackson before I leave.'

'What happened to Mr. Jackson?'

'He suffered a severe sprain to his ankle this evening. It is imperative he remain off his feet, but there is no one to care for him. The man is pugnacious! Stubborn! If I do not find someone to attend him, I know he will walk about, which could result in a permanent injury. I must send someone over to ensure he is taken care of. His last meal was at midday, so if I do not send someone to see to him right away, he is certain to ignore my instructions to remain seated and instead seek sustenance.'

Caroline drew back in disbelief at what the doctor was suggesting. 'Surely . . . I cannot, Dr. Hadley! I am a single woman. If I attend to a man in his home, my reputation will be utterly ruined!'

She could not help the thought that followed.

And I have been avoiding the handsome

blacksmith since the day we met! I cannot possibly be alone with him!

The doctor looked about, then back at the wagon where Mr. Bow sat with a tense expression, evidently concerned at the delay in returning to his wife's side.

Leaning in, Dr. Hadley lowered his voice. 'Rest assured, Mr. Bow is hard of hearing, and I shall be the only one who knows, and I swear I shall never breathe a word of it. I found a couple of people at the inn, but they were far too inebriated to be of use, and the innkeeper . . . he refused to help. Not that I would trust that man to care for anyone at the best of times. Everyone else is home with their family, and I do not have time to find someone else.'

Caroline shook her head. She wanted to assist, but this was too risky.

'Mrs. Brown, Mr. Jackson is a very important member of our community. Under ordinary circumstances, I could find any number of people willing to assist him. And he has many staff. But it is the holidays, and I am out of time.

Please, this is important! I have seen injuries like this become incurable maladies due to neglect. Mr. Jackson is yet a young man, a man who provides many people with work and is himself a highly skilled smith who helps our community by his own hand. I would hate for him to develop chronic problems with his leg when he was doing such a kind favour.'

'Dr. Hadley, if someone sees me entering his home, it could ruin my business. I would be run out of town.'

The doctor reached out, clasping her hand gently in his own to stare deep into her eyes. 'Mrs. Brown, I assure you it is the right thing to do. You can approach the house from the alley and enter through his back door. Mrs. Bow is having her first child, and I must get to her side immediately. I know it is a lot to ask . . .'

Caroline rubbed her free hand over her chin. She looked out on the deserted street. Hers was the only light to be seen, which was evidently how the doctor had found her. It could not do any harm. No one was about to see. As long as she was discreet, she could help the doctor, and she did not have a good reason to refuse. Hesitantly, she nodded.

Dr. Hadley squeezed her hand in gratitude. 'Thank you, Mrs. Brown. His cottage is near the end of the street, just past Mrs. Heeley's. You will know you have reached her house by the broken tiles and ladder in her backyard. If you can just take care of him until tomorrow night, I swear to it that no one will ever know you were there!'

The doctor dug in his pocket, pulling out a page and thrusting it into her hand. 'Here are my instructions for Mr. Jackson's care. I will call on him on Tuesday morning and bring one of his apprentices along to take care of him then.'

With that, Dr. Hadley turned to run over to the wagon, his great wool coat flapping in the night air as he hastily raised himself onto the seat next to Mr. Bow.

The farmer tipped his hat in greeting to Caroline, then prompted his horse forward. She watched as they started down the street through the falling snow, hoping that John Bow was oblivious to the specifics of the doctor's request or there would be too many people aware of where she was going tonight.

Locking the door, she read the doctor's scrawling handwriting as she considered what she might need to take with her. Making a mental list, she gathered her things, put out the candles, and headed to the back to find her cloak. She suspected it would be a long night, what with her and the blacksmith spending Christmas Eve together.

Alone.

Was the universe throwing temptation in her path to test her will? Certainly, by morning she would know if she had managed to transform herself into a chaste woman these past two years since her ill-advised indiscretions with Lord Saunton in the stables.

3

The Invasion

William woke from a doze, shaking his head to clear the fog. His ankle was thrumming something fierce, the relentless ache stealing away his energy and making rest nearly impossible. He supposed the dull pain might be the cause of his fatigue, sapping his strength bit by bit.

His front room was dark except for the glow of the fire, which was beginning to flicker and die. Soon, he would be without light. Shadows crept along the walls, stretching and fading as the embers crackled softly.

William sat up, setting off sharp twinges in his leg. Dr. Hadley had instructed him to recline on the settee and rest, promising to send over someone to assist him, but the doctor must have failed to locate anyone. William would need to get up and take care of himself. The prospect was unpleasant, but he was hardly the sort to sit idle when things needed doing.

He attempted to stand, then dropped back down with a hiss of pain and a muttered curse that would have made his mother frown. Huffing a deep sigh, he tried to think of what to do. The fire needed to be stoked, and he needed to eat if he was to maintain his strength. But his ankle was a fiery throb, and Dr. Hadley's admonition had been clear — he would take far longer to heal if he failed to stay off his feet.

It is obvious the doctor is not going to find someone willing to attend me on Christmas Eve, he thought grimly.

For the first time, William considered if his life choices were questionable. He might have built a successful smithy, but he had no family and no close friends. Now he sat injured during the holidays without a solitary person to assist him. Not one person was thinking of him this evening.

He rubbed his jaw, feeling the bristle of his beard against his palm. It was a sobering thought, one that lingered longer than he would have liked. His stomach growled loudly, as if to contribute its sentiments to the conversation he was having with himself.

With a loud groan, William fell back onto the settee and raised his legs back onto the arm. He would rise and tend to the fire, then find a meal in his kitchen, but for now, he just wanted to lie back and scowl at the ceiling, his thoughts swirling around his solitude.

He must have drifted off, for the next thing he knew, the click of a door handle startled him back to wakefulness. His eyes flew open, heart leaping in his chest. He heard the scrape of the back door opening and the sound of footsteps on the stone floor of his kitchen.

Someone huffed with exertion, followed by the unmistakable thud of something heavy being placed on the oak table where he ate his meals. William frowned. The doctor had found someone to send over?

Was it one of the boys who lived in the

cottage on the next street? Surely, it was not any of the men from the inn nearby. William muttered under his breath at the thought. Was his nocturnal visitor inebriated? The doctor had better sense than that . . . he hoped.

From the back, he could hear a candle being lit, a soft glow of light seeping through the doorway, casting long shadows along the floorboards.

'Mr. Jackson?'

William struggled back up to a seated position, surprise causing his heart to thud like a drum. It was a woman! But who . . .

Oh, no! No, no, no . . . Please, the doctor did not send —

'Mr. Jackson?'

It was her! Bathed in the light of the candle fitted into the holder she held in her hand. The glow accentuated her blonde hair, casting her lovely face in gentle shadows and illuminating her serene expression. The woman he had been avoiding these past weeks now stood in his home, like a ray of sunshine cutting through winter's gloom.

So much for maintaining my distance!

'Dr. Hadley sent me to tend to you. He said you are injured?'

William shook his head in dismay, stroking his beard while he tried to think. 'You cannot be here!'

Mrs. Brown ignored his protest, walking around the room to light more candles before setting down her candle-holder and taking up the fire poker to bank the fire. William watched, help-less and astonished, while savouring the cheeriness that she brought with her. The room, which had felt so dreary just moments before, now glowed with warmth and light, her presence lending it an unexpected brightness.

'Dr. Hadley impressed upon me the importance of your health to our little community, and assured me that no one would learn of my presence.' She poked at the coals expertly, sending sparks flut-tering upward. 'Do you know that the lock on your back door is broken? It does not catch properly.'

She came forward to stand before him. William scowled. 'What on earth are you wearing?'

He could hear his tone was barking, but he could not help it. Shock at her proximity — the woman who had been in his thoughts since their meeting the month before — warred with the pain in his leg and the impulse to maintain the privacy of his home. She was not merely attractive; she was a force to be reckoned with, an unwed woman who had launched a successful shop in an unfamiliar town and already made her mark. His fellow proprietors were speaking of her incessantly, which made it all the more difficult to push her from his thoughts. Having her in such close proximity was entirely unsettling to his carefully cultivated calm.

Mrs. Brown looked down at her cloak. 'It is a winter cloak.'

'It is decidedly not! There is no possibility that cloak keeps you warm in the winter. Why does it have such wide sleeves? There is nothing to prevent the chill!'

Mrs. Brown wrinkled her nose, an expression of irritation dancing across her features. 'It is beautiful, and I love it! I made it from the remnants of a coat my grandmother owned . . . After she died.'

The last was said with a sad intonation, and William experienced a pang of guilt. That was the trouble with Mrs. Brown — she made him feel things. Heaving an exasperated breath, he relented. 'I apologise. Show it to me.'

The modiste brightened up, mercurial in her shift of mood. 'I made it from green velvet and cut up my grandmother's coat to create this fur trimming.' She turned the lapel to show him the pale pelt that framed the velvet.

'And what of the sleeves?' he asked, eyebrows raised. The utterly impractical sleeves that could not possibly assist with the retention of heat on a cold winter's night!

Mrs. Brown held up one of her arms to display the deep fall. 'I saw something like it in a woodcutting of a woman in a medieval gown. It appealed to my romantic side.'

'Let me see it, then.'

She twirled, her skirts flaring slightly as she spun. Despite how impractical the garment was, William had to admit — if only to himself — that she looked enchanting in the dark green velvet and pale fur with the wide hood framing her face. The firelight flickered, catching the softness of the fur and the rich sheen of the velvet, lending her an almost ethereal glow.

Mrs. Brown was a personification of Christmas, all warmth and bright cheerfulness in the midst of winter's chill. When she came to a stop, his gaze, unbidden, drifted to her mouth — the gentle curve of her lips that had lingered in his thoughts far longer than was sensible. Despite his discomfort, he imagined standing up to take her hands and draw her close, to hold her and simply bask in the lightness she seemed to carry with her. He shook the thought away immediately. Preposterous!

Mrs. Brown frowned, apparently noticing something odd about his expression. 'Mr. Jackson, I must insist you lie back down and rest as the doctor instructed.'

With a long sigh, he shifted and settled back against the settee's arm, stretching out his legs once more. He would never state it aloud, but it was gratifying to raise his leg, which diminished the persistent throbbing.

'Your cloak is lovely,' he admitted roughly. 'But, Mrs. Brown, I need your assurance that you would not venture out into a cold snap with such a garment. You would be chilled to the bone with such gaping cuffs.'

Mrs. Brown chuckled softly, the sound gentle and sincere. 'I work all the time, and then race home to my rooms. There is no possibility of my freezing out in the cold.'

'Nevertheless, Mrs. Brown — '

'If we are to spend Christmas together, perhaps it would be easier to call me Caroline?'

William's breath caught, and he stared

at her, unblinking, for the span of a moment before he remembered to take air.

Caroline.

It was wonderfully fitting for such an exquisite and accomplished woman. The name suited her, bright and warm, with a touch of elegance.

After several seconds of silence, he realised Mrs. Br — Caroline was gazing at him expectantly.

'You may call me William.'

This was going to be a very long night. Caroline's presence filled the room with an unexpected warmth, and he found himself oddly grateful for it. To hear her voice cutting through the silence. To see her smile brighten the dark corners of his solitary life.

William exhaled deeply, fighting back the strange fluttering in his chest.

'How did you injure yourself . . . William?'

There was a hesitancy to how she formed his name on her lips. William shot her a glance, observing how her eyes skittered away, and he realised the young woman was as nervous as he at this unexpected interlude of theirs.

'It was nothing. Just a mishap with my ladder. I spend little time at home, so my tools here are not well maintained like the ones in the smithy. It turned out to be a mistake to use them without inspection.'

'Huh. So nothing to do with the roof repairs at Mrs. Heeley's cottage?'

William scowled. She was far too observant. 'How did you know that?'

'I saw the broken ladder and tiles out back. It was very kind of you to help the widow. Did she ask you to take care of it on Christmas Eve for a particular reason? Would it not have been easier with the help of one of your men?'

William mumbled his reply in a resentful tone.

'What was that?'

He frowned before admitting the truth in a louder voice. 'Mrs. Heeley did not ask. You are not to mention it to her. I need to have one of my apprentices clean up the clutter so she will not learn of it, or it will embarrass her that I interceded.'

'You secretly repaired her roof on Christmas Eve?' William heard the note of awed admiration in Caroline's voice, and a strange warmth settled in his chest. It stirred something gentle and unfamiliar, a flicker of pride at having been noticed by her.

They might be spending the holidays together, but there was no reason to become too familiar. He admired her far too much already, and he did not wish to grow fonder of her than he already had. The notion was uncomfortable, and he tore his gaze away, scowling at the ceiling. 'Are you going to make something to eat, or what?'

A soft, melodic chuckle was her only response. William listened as her footsteps pattered out of the room, the urge to call her back almost overpowering. Almost.

* * *

Caroline chuckled as she made her way back to the kitchen. The blacksmith might be grim and full of bluster, but he had just revealed his soft side. He had injured himself doing secret repairs for the old woman next door. Mr. Jacks — William was kind beneath all that cantankerous posturing.

She had to admit to her relief that the man was currently confined to the settee. William was far less imposing now that he was not towering over her like a great wall of muscle and sinew, forged from years of beating iron and steel into shape. He looked almost approachable lying there, his large frame stretched out with an air of reluctant surrender.

William.

It suited him. A strong English name for a strong English man.

She could not deny the flicker of awareness, but given that the man was relegated to lying on his back, she was confident she could maintain her composure. All she had to do was get through the night without incident, and she would know that she had found her footing — and her moral backbone — around handsome men.

Granted, William was not as polished or charming like Lord Saunton, the man who had proven her character to be flawed. But he was just as compelling, if not more so. Caroline supposed this evening would be a test of her mettle. Fortunately, the man was laid up and in no position to cause her nerves any distress.

Humming a Christmas carol, she set water to boil. Scrounging around the kitchen, she located his tea things and decided to make the blacksmith a sandwich. She would prepare something more substantial in the morning, but for tonight, it would be best to feed him as quickly as possible.

She sliced the fresh bread she found, adding generous layers of cheese and smoked ham before laying it out neatly on a plate. Then she cut a much smaller sandwich for herself. Digging through her basket, she pulled out the York biscuits and rolled wafers she had bought from Mr. Andrews earlier that day. She doubted that a man like William would prefer milk in his tea, so she poured two cups, leaving his plain while adding a little milk to her own.

Picking up the laden tray, still humming, Caroline walked back to the sitting room.

William lay stretched out on the settee, his eyes shut. Now that there was more light in the room, Caroline noted a pallor to his bronzed skin. The man clearly needed to eat.

Walking over, she placed the tray down on the table between the settees before taking a seat across from him. William slowly opened his eyes, his blue gaze falling to the tray, and an expression of raw hunger flashed across his face. He pushed himself up to lean against the padded arm, his stomach growling loudly at the mere sight of food.

'Thank you . . . Caroline.'

The sound of her name on his lips sent a shiver down her spine. His voice was low and gentle, completely at odds with his usual gruffness. William had sculpted, smooth lips — something she had not been able to help noticing on the day they met — and she found herself imagining that they would be warm when he spoke her name again.

There will be no foolishness, Caroline!

Her eyelids fluttered as she chased the thoughts from her mind. Lifting the plate with his thick-cut sandwich, she handed it over with a nod of acknowledgment, then moved his teacup so he could reach it easily.

She picked up her own tea to sip, lifting her sandwich to take a delicate bite before setting it back down. Peeking from beneath her lashes, she observed him devouring his sandwich. He took up his tea and drank deeply, the scalding liquid clearly no deterrent. She supposed that as a blacksmith, he was well accustomed to heat. With satisfaction, she watched the colour return to his cheeks as he ate, the tightness around his eyes easing somewhat.

Now that she was finally off her feet, Caroline glanced around the room. Above the fireplace hung a seascape of a calm day on the water, tiny boats bobbing under a bright sun whilst waves crashed onto the rocks at the foot of a cliff. Between the comfortable, overstuffed settees lay a rug woven in blues and greens, and several plump pillows in similar hues decorated them. Across the room, tucked into the corner near the staircase, was a small wooden table and four chairs with matching seat cushions.

'Your cottage is not what I expected,' she remarked, her gaze drifting back to him.

William looked up from his meal, shrugging his broad shoulders, the movement causing the firelight to flicker across his frame. Caroline suppressed the flutter of awareness that rippled through her. 'I have not redecorated it since I took it over. Aunt Gertrude is from Cornwall.' He gestured to the painting.

'I like it,' she assured him, offering a gentle smile before continuing her meal.

After taking several bites of her own sandwich, she finally stood. Taking his teacup to refill it, she made her way back to the kitchen. Returning to William, she found him chewing on a York biscuit with an expression of pure bliss. He nodded his thanks when she placed the cup down. The biscuit looked tiny in his large hand, and the sight of it brought up thoughts of —

No, Caroline!

Chastising herself, she retreated to the kitchen. With determination, she took up the supplies she had brought and returned to the front room. Setting her bundle down, she grabbed one of the chairs in the corner and dragged it to the window, ignoring the curious look William sent her way.

'What are you doing?'

'I am making your home festive.'

'You brought Christmas boughs to attend to me?' The man appeared genuinely perplexed as Caroline sat down with the boughs in her lap and began to tie one to the windowsill.

'Why not? We are stuck together for Christmas, and there is no one at my shop to appreciate these. They are wonderful, are they not? Mrs. Greer made them for me.' Caroline breathed deeply of the rosemary scent as she worked, the fresh, wintry fragrance filling the room with a bit of cheer. She did not miss the quizzical look William threw in her direction. He clearly thought she was a madwoman, dressing his home with Christmas greenery. But if work kept her hands busy and prevented her imagination from wandering to unwelcome places, then William was about to have the most festive home in all of Chatternwell.

Good heavens, he is a handsome man!

Not in the polished manner of Lord Saunton, who was undoubtedly one of the most elegant men she had ever laid eyes on. No, William Jackson possessed a different sort of handsomeness — a rugged, earthy kind that spoke of strength and honest labour. He was not crafted for ballrooms but for the anvil and the forge, and there was something admirable in that. His broad shoulders and powerful frame were honed by years of hard work, his hands marked by calluses earned through dedication.

His white shirt gaped slightly, revealing the strong column of his throat, and his waistcoat had been set aside, leaving him in just his shirtsleeves. One stocking was missing, and she caught a glimpse of a muscled calf dusted with hair where his breeches rode up. Caroline quickly tore her gaze away, feeling warmth creep up her cheeks.

This is simply a test, Caroline! You are to prove you have matured into a sensible woman, she reminded herself firmly.

Clearing her throat, she resumed humming her carol while her fingers worked on the boughs. What a relief that she had brought something to do! Even now she could feel his eyes watching her, but she paid him no mind. Once she was done with this, she had more work to occupy herself with. She would prepare a poultice for his ankle following the doctor's instructions, then tidy the kitchen. If she kept herself occupied, she could get through the evening unscathed.

Caroline's eyes widened in sudden horror, her humming halted. She had not considered where she would be sleeping that night. William would likely remain on the settee since the narrow, steep flight of stairs would be impossible with his swollen ankle. But where did that leave her?

Biting her lip, she glanced around the sitting room, her fingers ceasing to work until she glimpsed the second settee. It was large enough for her to rest upon, though not terribly comfortable.

Across the room, William followed her gaze and, for the first time since she had met him, a smile spread across his face. It was devastating — a flash of white teeth startling in contrast to his dark beard — and Caroline found herself struggling for breath as she focused on the lips she had noticed before. It was not often he smiled, but when he did, it transformed his entire face, softening the harshness of his features.

'You are wondering where you will sleep?'

Speechless, her tongue tied by her embarrassing thoughts, all she could do was nod.

'Perhaps before you decide that, you might want to draw the curtains.' He gestured to the window where she was working.

Stricken, Caroline spun her head round to stare out at the deserted street in dismay. She could only hope no one had walked by. Standing in haste, Christmas boughs scattering to the floor, she jerked the blue curtains shut and then hurried to the other window to shut those as well.

There she stood, hands clasped before her, cheeks flushed with mortification.

'No one saw you.' William's husky voice broke the silence.

'Are you certain?'

'I am. I have had a clear view of the windows since you walked within view. Caroline . . . I want you to know that if any of this damages your reputation . . . I would do the right thing.'

Caroline stopped breathing. That was the last thing she had expected to hear. In all her years, no man had ever offered such a thing. Even if it was merely to protect her reputation, it was still . . . noble.

The attractive blacksmith, who secretly took care of old ladies, was now offering to be a gentleman and marry her if her reputation suffered? She did not need any more reasons to admire the man. Her thoughts drifted, unbidden, to the notion of what it would be like to be his wife. To sit across from him at the breakfast table. To see him coming in from the forge, his sleeves rolled up, hair tousled from the day's work.

'You want to . . . marry me?'

Several seconds passed, the crackle of the fire the only sound breaking the silence. Finally, he replied, his reluctance evident. 'I would prefer not to marry, but if it were required, we could come to an arrangement.'

Caroline slowly resumed breathing.

'I . . . appreciate it. But as you said, no one was out there to witness my presence.'

Had he just offered to marry the woman?

William shook his head slowly after Caroline left the room, mumbling something about preparing a poultice. What a foolish thing to say. Yet, he supposed he would do it — if it came to that. He could not stand by and allow a fine woman of Caroline's quality to suffer harm for doing him a good deed. He could not allow it for any woman, but especially not the lovely mantua-maker — *modiste*, he corrected himself — who had impressed his fellow townsfolk with her skill and industry.

Life had taken an odd turn since the day he first saw her beckoning little Annie Greer into her shop. He never would have imagined himself learning the difference between a modiste and a mantua-maker, yet here he was, thinking of it.

From the kitchen, he heard her begin

to hum again. The tune was familiar — cheerful, light-hearted. So was she. Her alarm at discovering the curtains still open had at first seemed amusing, but it had swiftly turned serious. The fear on her face — genuine fear — had struck him like a hammer. It was easy for a man to forget how dangerous even the appearance of impropriety could be for a woman alone. And for a woman in trade, her livelihood could vanish with one misplaced whisper.

He lay back and closed his eyes, letting the hum of her voice blend with the sound of boiling water. The quiet movement in the kitchen, the gentle melody — these things soothed him more than he expected. He had long dreaded the holidays for the memories they brought. But having someone here, even for a day, was a strange comfort.

Just for tonight. Tomorrow she will be gone.

Caroline returned with the poultice supplies on a tray. She set them on the table and took a seat, her movements gentle and purposeful. The doctor had removed William's stocking earlier, so she now unwound the bandage with delicate care. Her humming continued, a balm in itself.

'I am sorry you have to spend your holidays nursing me,' William said quietly.

Her hazel eyes met his. 'It is quite all right, William. I was working, as it happens.'

A faint smile touched his mouth, though it saddened him that a woman such as she — so capable, so warm — should be alone this night. She ought to be surrounded by children and laughter, not tending to a surly blacksmith.

She wrinkled her nose as she dipped cloth into warm vinegar. 'My word, the spirits in this mixture are strong! Quite enough to take one's breath away.'

He tried not to flinch as she applied the compress to his swollen ankle. 'What is it?'

'The poultice? The doctor recommended vinegar, oatmeal, camphorated spirits of wine, Mindererus's spirit, volatile liniment, volatile aromatic spirit — diluted, of course — and the common fomentation. With brandy.'

He blinked. 'My word. Did I even have all those things?'

She grinned. 'No. I found four, maybe five. Hopefully, it will suffice.'

'I am sure it will. Dr. Hadley said the key was to rest it. He had me soak it in ice water first thing.'

'There you are, then. A poultice now, a bandage, and rest. You should be well on your way to mending by the end of Christmastide.'

He looked at her thoughtfully. 'Are you always such an optimist?'

Her hands paused in their task. Something shadowed her features for a moment before she spoke. 'I find it helps to count blessings. The world can be a lonely place. But if you make a habit of noticing what is good . . . you can be happier.'

He was quiet for a long moment.

'And what blessings would you count

for me? Now that I have made a mess of things.' He gestured towards his ankle.

'You are a respected tradesman with a successful smithy. The doctor trusts you enough to worry over your care. You are strong and in generally good health. And' — her voice softened — 'you have your whole life ahead of you.'

William stared at her. She spoke with such conviction, her face alight with sincerity, her eyes gentle and earnest. She meant every word.

He was suddenly struck by the realization that she was unlike anyone he had met. She did not flatter. She believed in people. A warmth sparked in his chest. It frightened him. The sudden impulse to reach for her, to hold her close, to simply feel again . . . it was too much.

'Are you nearly done?' he asked, more sharply than he intended.

She flinched. Her hands stilled, and he saw her withdraw into herself.

'I shall bind the poultice when I have cleared away,' she said softly.

She stood and left the room, and

William stared at the spot where she had been. Guilt rose bitterly in his throat. He had wounded her with those careless words, but what choice did he have? It was safer this way. He could not allow himself to want things that were not meant for him.

He had once persuaded his cousin Charles to join him in the fight against Bonaparte. Then Charles had died at the end of a bayonet, and William had been the one to return and tell his uncle and aunt they would never see their only son again. He had watched their grief tear them apart. And worse — he had delivered the news to Charles's betrothed, who had clung to him and wept with a brokenness he would never forget.

No. He could not risk anyone else. Certainly not someone like Caroline, who brought light wherever she went.

He lay back again, the pain in his ankle a dull throb compared to the ache in his chest. In the kitchen, she worked quietly. No humming. No words.

Good. He could not afford sunshine.

Not when he had long since resigned himself to shadows.

Some time later, she returned. She wore a modest night rail with a pale wrap embroidered with tiny, careful stitches. Her hair was plaited and tied with a primrose ribbon. Likely her own work. The thought settled uncomfortably within him.

She knelt to bind the poultice, then spread a blanket over him without a word. It was not yet late, but fatigue pressed down on him. Still, as she moved about the room to snuff the candles, his eyes followed her. She carried herself with quiet dignity, her movements unhurried and graceful. When she finally settled on the second settee, William let his eyes fall shut. It was safer to sleep.

4
The Past

William opened his eyes to find himself once more at Château d'Hougoumont.

It was right about noon, with the sun beating down on the quagmire of mud left in the rainstorm's wake earlier that morning, when the north gate was breached. A sous-lieutenant of the French First Light Infantry broke through the gate with an axe, enabling bluecoats to pour into the fortified courtyard that William's regiment had been charged with defending.

William frantically sought his cousin's position, yelling his name, when he caught sight of Charles near the gate. From thirty feet away, William raced forward to assist him, but he was too late. He could only watch helplessly as Charles was run through with a flashing steel bayonet, falling to the ground as if time itself had slowed down to drag out William's agonising futility.

For the span of a second, William was

frozen as grief slammed into his body, almost bringing him to his knees. Even at this distance, there was no doubt his cousin was dead, with his empty eyes staring into the abyss.

But then the tide of French soldiers reached him. Realising there was no time to reload his musket, he raised it up to fight, as he had been taught weeks ago when Charles and he had signed up to fight Boney. That was when he noticed that his bayonet was missing. William saw the soldiers were upon him, and he had no method to defend himself.

Recalling the training sergeant had said that Brown Bess had a thick stock and would not break if he used it as a club, William's instincts as a blacksmith spurred him into motion while a mindless rage washed over him in a tide of red. They had killed his cousin, his best friend.

If I am to die in the yard today, I will take as many Frenchmen down with me as I can!

William raised his musket like a forge hammer, swinging it down with the force and precision of a smith beating iron on his anvil. Cracking it down, he raised it once more and swung it down. And raised it and swung again. And again.

When William's rage slowly dissipated, he was panting from his exertions. He groggily returned to his senses from the anger and hatred that had engulfed his mind, to find that he now stood with dead French soldiers at his feet. The north gate was closed, and his fellow redcoats were frantically fighting the remaining enemy left within the yard.

It was like this every night. Every relentless night since the Battle of Waterloo. This was the part of his recurring nightmare when he threw back his head to roar all the pain, and loss, and regret shuddering through him. Charles was dead, and William had killed five men in close combat with the skills of his livelihood turned to abhorrent violence. He did not even know the men's names. Would never know their names. Or if they had wives, children, parents who would grieve them.

This was the precise moment he would now make his vow to —

Then he heard it, a melodic voice humming a Christmas carol.

Thus spoke the angel. Suddenly
appeared a shining throng
of angels praising God, who thus
addressed their joyful song:
'All glory be to God on high,
and to the earth be peace;
to those on whom his favor rests
goodwill shall never cease.'

He frowned, hesitating, uncertain of what to make of the joyful holiday song here in this yard of death.

This was a fresh development. He had suffered this nightmare for more than five years. It had never deviated before. Every night, it was the same sequence of events. Over and over again, so that he was afraid to fall asleep. Afraid to revisit this yard.

William shook his head in befuddlement, then turned to discover the source of the song.

Approaching him was sunshine herself, draped in a flowing white gown. Her blonde hair was lit, her face serene as she walked towards him, paying no mind to the carnage at her feet. She sang as she neared him, and somehow the soldiers parted to let her through so she might come to a stop in front of him.

Caroline Brown looked up into his eyes and asked, 'Did you count your blessings, William?'

'Blessings?' he echoed dumbly.

She shook her head at him, as if admonishing a forgetful child. 'Life is hard. Counting your blessings makes it easier to find happiness in this world.'

His brow creased, and he found himself at a genuine loss as he stared down at his filthy pale pantaloons and muddy boots, while breathing in the stench of blood and gunpowder. Surely this was a jest? There was no possibility of hope or optimism to be found in a hell like this. Caroline could not possibly have any blessings of value to share with him.

'What blessings are to be found in this farmyard of death?'

Her pink lips curled into a smile, and William wondered if he was missing some vital clue. She seemed confident there was grace present. 'There are always blessings to be counted. It is all about perspective.'

She held out a hand, and it was clean. And soft. And perfect. He did not wish to sully her by taking hold of it, but she merely stood there, waiting with a tilt of her head until he reluctantly reached out to clasp it. 'Come with me, blacksmith.'

Leading him over to a fortified wall, she stepped up onto a barrel with his help, then gestured for him to take his place at her side. Gingerly, he climbed up and turned to where she was peering with a fascinated expression.

William's eyes widened in amazement as he realised he was watching himself. Events unfolded once more, but this time he watched them from the side. He was no longer a participant in the battle.

The French sous-lieutenant broke through the north gate, wielding his steel axe in a triumphant charge.

Bluecoats followed him, flooding into the courtyard.

William watched once more in torment as Charles was run through with a bayonet, this vantage point a new seat to witness hell unfolding yet again.

Then William watched himself across the yard as he called out his cousin's name in agony. He witnessed the other William's anguish, followed by the realisation he had no bayonet with which to defend himself as the tide of blue rushed towards him. The other William brought the musket back over his head to wield it in the manner of a blacksmith's hammer.

Caroline was humming next to him, nudging him and pointing to the left of where William was fighting the enemy.

Curious about what had her attention, he focused on where she pointed and noticed for the first time that as he fought, Corporal Graham, Graham's brother, and several soldiers were fighting near him while Captain Wyndham led them to the north gate. As the other William brought the stock of his musket down on the head of a French soldier, he now noticed that the man had been preparing to stab Corporal Graham from behind with the point of his bayonet.

The corporal paid no heed to what was

happening behind him as William cracked his stock down on the enemy soldier's skull, killing him in a single, powerful blow. Graham raised his musket and fired at a French sniper who was taking aim at Captain Wyndham. He hit the sniper, and then the group of redcoats fought their way forward under the command of Lieutenant Colonel MacDonell to the north gate. Closing the gate was their only hope of survival, and the men fought their way valiantly in service of the British Army, as they had been instructed to do. Château d'Hougoumont had to be defended at any cost.

William watched on, realising for the first time that while he fought in the skirmish across the yard, his fellow redcoats made it back to the gate and struggled to get it closed. Then they turned to fight the remaining bluecoats in the yard.

Caroline broke off from her song. 'If you had not been standing in that exact spot, Corporal Graham might have died. If he had died, so too would Captain Wyndham have died. And if Captain Wyndham had died, Lieutenant Colonel MacDonell would have failed, and Hougoumont would have fallen.'

'What of it?' William heard the belligerence in his voice, but he could not help it. He had returned to the site of his downfall as he did every horrible night. It was hell on earth, and he had had to relive it every evening since that day.

Caroline turned to gaze at him with lively hazel eyes. 'It was a blessing you were here that day, William. The Duke of Wellington himself declared that the success of the battle turned upon the closing of the gates at Hougoumont.'

William's brows drew together in his confusion. He supposed he must have known that, considering Caroline was merely a guest in his dream. She could not point it out unless he had already heard it. At least, that seemed the most logical explanation.

Observing his perplexity, Caroline placed her hand on his forearm in a gesture of comfort as she explained, 'If you had not been there to stop that Frenchman from stabbing Corporal Graham, we might have lost the entire war with Napoleon.'

That seemed far-fetched. And besides, it did not address the excruciating cause of his true grief. 'But because of me, Charles is dead!'

'Charles was going to sign up whether you joined him or not. He was frustrated that more than a decade of war with Boney looked to be starting anew. He wanted no more wives of Chatternwell to be widowed. When Boney escaped, Charles informed you that he would fight with or without you because he was a good man. A courageous man.'

William paused, thinking back on the events leading up to Hougoumont. Now that he thought about it, Charles had been the first to raise the subject of joining the fight after Boney escaped Elba.

'Charles would be proud of the part he played that day. That his loss prompted you to fly into a rage, which in turn led to saving the corporal. His presence here that day, it was — '

'A blessing?'

Caroline smiled. 'Indeed. We did not need any more fatherless children in Chatternwell because of the little tyrant's quest for power. Charles had a choice in his fate because he was allowed to grow into a man. He had a mother and father who loved him, and he chose to honour them by protecting the liberty of England.'

William sat down, his knees no longer able to hold him up as he altered his perspective of the past. He had lived in regret for five long years, but would he have done anything differently? Would he have convinced Charles to stay home, never himself signed up, based on what he knew now?

'Regretting the past is a waste of time, William. We must count the blessings and then continue with our lives.'

Caroline had taken a seat beside him, her white skirts blinding in the sunlight as she placed her delicate hand over his. 'Charles would want his sacrifice to be meaningful. He would want to know that his memory lived on through you.'

The chains that had bound him since that day at the fields of Waterloo slowly loosened their hold and the weight of them melted away. As the tight bands disappeared,

William felt his eyes welling with moisture. Raising his hand, he found tears streaming down as he quietly accepted the past and released his guilt.

Next to him, Caroline resumed her melodic humming as he finally wept for his cousin's death but understood that it had played an important role within a hitherto unknown master plan.

⋆ ⋆ ⋆

When William's eyes flickered open, he was surprised to find his cheeks were wet. A strange discovery — for he must have wept like a babe in his sleep. The room slowly came into focus as the dream faded.

He flinched when he realised Caroline was standing over him, her hand resting gently on his arm as if to wake him. A candle flickered on the table beside her, casting golden light upon her worried face. She was stroking his arm in a soothing gesture.

'William! Thank heavens you are

awake! You were having a nightmare, and I could not rouse you.'

He blinked, struggling to clear the lingering haze of sleep from his eyes.

'How did you know? What was I doing?'

'You were highly agitated — growling and flailing in your sleep — and then you . . .' Her voice softened, clearly hesitant to finish. 'You were weeping?'

William swallowed hard and slowly lifted himself to lean back against the arm of the settee. 'I was counting my blessings.'

'And that made you' — Caroline faltered, apparently reluctant to wound his pride — 'cry?'

He paused to consider how best to explain what had happened. 'I discovered that counting blessings can stir emotions that have long lain buried. I was grieving my past . . . and releasing my failings. You were there.'

She drew back slightly, surprise flickering in her expression. 'In your nightmare?'

'It was a nightmare. One I have experienced frequently, but then you arrived, and it . . . changed. Your words stayed with me. I saw events from a new vantage.'

'It was good that I was there, then?'

'Very good,' he said, his voice rough but sincere.

Something had shifted deep within him. For the first time in years, he felt a measure of peace. Caroline's gentle counsel before he had drifted off had followed him into sleep, and her dream-self had guided him through memories he had never dared revisit.

Charles would not have wished for me to grieve forever.

This woman — who smelled faintly of beeswax and rosemary, who had offered him sustenance and warmth — had done what no other had managed in five long years. She had pierced the veil of guilt that clouded his soul.

He let his gaze drift downward, noting how her wrap had slipped slightly, revealing the delicate fabric of her night rail. He looked away at once, a flush of awareness prickling at the nape of his neck. When his eyes returned, they settled on her face — on the soft, expressive curve of her lips — and he found himself wondering, fleetingly, whether she still thought of the tea and biscuits they had shared earlier that evening.

Then, quite without intending to, his thoughts strayed to how comforting it might be to draw her close — to rest, simply, in the gentle solace of her presence, to feel the calm she brought with her, and, perhaps, just perhaps, to breathe in the quiet sweetness of her nearness.

* * *

Caroline watched as William's gaze settled on her lips, his expression shifting into something unreadable. He drew in a breath, and his tongue briefly touched his lower lip, as though lost in thought.

She recognised the flicker of interest now playing across his features, the faint flush rising in his cheeks. Beginning to edge away, her pulse fluttered, a warm awareness blooming in her veins, just as the blacksmith grinned — an expression so rare and startling it revealed a flash of white teeth. He certainly appeared more amiable than she had ever seen him, his usual grim air replaced by something far more approachable.

And, if she were truthful, even more appealing.

No men, Caroline! No men!

Yet she found herself momentarily caught by the depth in his gaze. The desire to be near him — to feel the quiet strength he seemed to exude — was unexpectedly stirring.

The air tingled, like the crackle of static from brushing woollen garments. She continued to step back, but in her surprise, she had delayed too long.

A strong hand reached out — not rough, but firm — and closed gently around her wrist, guiding her forward until she came to rest lightly against him.

* * *

William leaned up, his lips brushing hers, and a warmth kindled between them. It was not fire, not fury, but something deep and steady — like the comforting glow of a hearth on a winter's night. He tasted her — tea and peppermint — and felt her lips respond, soft with surprise, then assured in return.

Their mouths met again, deepening not with urgency but with a quiet understanding that made his chest ache. She was real. Present. Glorious. And, for a moment, his.

His fingers slid into her hair, carefully loosening the plait, letting the silken length tumble free. He brought a handful to his face and inhaled deeply.

Vanilla. And peppermint.

My word . . . she is not merely the embodiment of sunshine — she is Christmastide itself.

She was in his arms. Warm, yielding, and real. The way she leaned into him, her lips moving with his as though she had longed for this — unspoken and true — it unraveled him.

Through the thin linen of his shirt, he could feel her nearness — her care. His hands cupped her face, brushing her cheeks, tracing the elegant line of her jaw, reverent in their motion.

Caroline's fingers slipped into his hair, tentative, then surer, and a breath escaped him — a sound more of wonder than of want. His body ached, not with hunger, but with something far fuller. Hope.

She had unlocked something in him. With her gentleness and her laughter, her grace and quiet resilience, she had drawn him out from the shadows of himself.

William wrapped his arms about her, drawing her gently close. They kissed again — slowly, reverently. He pressed his face to her neck, breathing her in. One hand traced the curve of her back, the other cradling her head.

Her name fell from his lips like a prayer. 'Caroline . . .'

And then, as if sensing the line neither wished to cross, he stilled. His breath came unevenly, his heart thudding against hers, and he rested his forehead to hers, close, but unmoving.

The warmth within him burned steady and clear, yet he made no move to take more.

Instead, he cupped her face once more and whispered, 'You bring me peace. And I would not wish to ruin that.'

* * *

In a daze, Caroline realised William was no longer kissing her. His head was rolled back on the settee arm as he panted for air, holding her head tenderly to him with a large hand that covered most of her crown. He was so powerful; she felt like a delicate fawn in his arms.

Listening to the thudding of his heart in his chest, she was amazed at what had just happened. She had never felt such closeness, scarcely able to grasp that he had stopped. Was he regretting their embrace? Or was he attempting to be a gentleman, halting his attentions at the edge of the wall of chastity she had spent years building?

Caroline did not know what to think. Her test of her resilience had not proven her moral fortitude had improved these past years, but she could not bring herself to regret the precious, stolen moments in William's arms. She knew the regret would come, but not yet. Not while she listened to the fire crackle and his heart thunder. This — this closeness — was the nearest she had ever come to contentment.

As their breath gradually slowed, Caroline realised it was time to rise and break their embrace. How had such a fine specimen of manhood remained unmarried? Why was he not husband to an attractive young woman with several children already? She guessed he was a few years older than herself; old enough to be settled, and young enough to enjoy it.

If William was married, you would not be in his arms on Christmas Eve.

She shut her eyes in painful regret.

That might not be true, given her past mistakes.

With that reminder, the past came rushing back, and Caroline recalled why she must stay away from virile men. She was not to be trusted. She did not trust herself.

Caroline gently pressed her palms to his chest and eased away, rising from the warmth of his arms. William let her go, and she could not decide whether to feel grateful or bereft.

Blast, this was why she stayed away from men. Because she turned into a dithering twit, as Lord Saunton had proved, and did stupid things just because she received a tidbit of male attentions.

She walked across the room and stood in front of the hearth, staring into the flames as if the answers to her character might be found flickering among the embers.

At last, she found her voice. 'Would you like some tea?'

Truly? That is the first thing you could find to say?

Caroline squared her shoulders. It was the proper thing to say. Her voice had been calm, giving no hint of the inner turmoil lashing at her. She ought to behave as if nothing had occurred and simply carry out the task the doctor had entrusted her with.

Why did the holiday season dredge up so many private longings? If only it were a normal day, she could work on her walking dress and restore her equilibrium. On a normal day, the doctor would have found someone else to attend William Jackson, and she would not now be confronted with the humiliating truth that she remained the same flawed girl who had made a ruinous mistake two years ago. She had not matured at all. No, she had simply avoided situations where her poor judgement could do further damage.

No men, no opportunities to betray my friends. No friends, no risk of losing their regard.

Work was the only answer. Work kept her focused. Work kept her safe from herself.

William's voice, hoarse and roughened by emotion, broke the silence. 'That would be appreciated.'

Caroline gave a short nod and left the room to prepare the tea.

* * *

William had kissed the modiste.

Yet, he could not find it in him to regret it. She had resuscitated his dead heart and made it beat again. It was as though he had been a corpse walking for five years and suddenly awakened to discover an entire world of possibility.

He was grateful she had moved away and offered the tea, because the truth was, he was currently overcome. After years of detachment, he did not know what to do with the powerful feelings surging inside him. He needed time — time to accustom himself to this altered perspective.

What a revelation it was to discover that he had been punishing himself needlessly. He agreed with the dream version of Caroline — he would best honour Charles's memory not through endless sorrow, but by respecting his cousin's sacrifice and building a future while carrying him within his heart. But what did that mean?

Where do I go from here?

He had broken off the kiss because he did not know what path he was careering down. His soul had cried out at the interruption, yearning to remain in the arms of the remarkable woman who had opened his eyes. Who had spoken with such bright conviction and offered him hope, without realising what her words would set into motion.

He needed to find his footing again.

This future that now stretched before him must be considered carefully. He could not involve another person — especially not someone like Caroline — in the midst of his confusion. He owed her more than a half-hearted affection born of gratitude and recent awakening.

But holding her had been an unadulterated delight. The kind of moment that settled into a man's bones and never left. Still, it would not be fair to her. He had no plans to court or wed — not now. Not when he had only just stepped out of the prison of grief and guilt. After five long years, he had found his freedom. He needed to live in it a while before making any promises he might come to question. She had shown him what was possible, but the path ahead must be walked alone for now.

And what a question it was — what paths lay open?

His business was thriving, largely due to the very single-mindedness that had kept him emotionally numb. He was not lacking in income or resources. The issue was not whether he could change course, but rather how.

Perhaps he might travel. He could visit the fields of Waterloo to pay proper respects to his cousin's memory. Or explore Italy and take in the ruins of Ancient Rome. He could even journey to the Americas, where he might begin again in a new land with no shadows of his past.

It was a marvel, really. Mere hours ago, he had clung to numbness like armour, unwilling to risk any feeling at all. And now he stood at a crossroads — one he had not imagined even in his wildest dreams. Apparently, changing one's mind could happen in an instant.

Or in a recurring nightmare . . . interrupted by a woman who brought light and vanilla and evergreen boughs into his quiet life.

She had no idea what her quiet strength had done. She had no idea the gift she had given him with her simple, profound advice:

Count your blessings.

And for the first time in five years, William Jackson had.

5
The Present

Caroline was humming her carol in the kitchen.

William was pleased to hear the soft melody. It was a comfort, that sign of her returned good spirits as she boiled water and moved around the back room. The sound of her presence — so capable, so quietly cheerful — soothed the unsettled edges within him.

Soon she returned with a tea tray, which included the rolled wafers she had given him earlier. He pushed himself more upright, careful of his leg, so he might drink, while Caroline perched on the table and gently explored the swelling at his ankle with cool fingertips.

'The swelling appears reduced,' she said with satisfaction, before rising with her cup and saucer and moving back to the other settee.

William shifted uncomfortably. There was now a pressing matter he could no longer ignore. He grimaced as he set his tea aside, trying to work out how to approach the issue with a measure of dignity.

Caroline must have noticed the movement — her expression flickered with realization. Without a word, she stood and crossed the room. William watched her go, lips twisting as he braced himself for discomfort — then brightened when he heard the gentle creak of the stairs. She had understood.

Shortly, she returned and crossed over to him, placing a chamber pot discreetly on the floor beside the settee. Without meeting his eye, she turned and quietly exited, closing the door behind her. William exhaled a long breath of relief. With a few cautious exertions, he managed the necessary task and eventually repositioned himself with some difficulty back onto the settee.

'You can return!' he called out once decently settled.

The door opened, and Caroline re-entered holding a bowl of water and some cloths. Without comment, she set the bowl on the table, moistened a cloth, and handed it to him. William accepted it with gratitude. The water was warm, and he used it to wash his hands, then placed the cloth on the tea tray. She handed him another, which he used to mop his face and neck.

'Thank you.'

'Not at all. I should have thought of it before. You have been trapped here for hours.'

Caroline resumed her place on the other settee and sipped her tea. William crunched into a wafer, grateful for the quiet civility between them. They sat for a time in companionable silence, the fire crackling softly as the storm beyond the windows thickened with snow. Eventually, William broke the quiet with a question that had lingered in his mind since the day they met.

'Why did you move to Chatternwell, Caroline?'

Her brow furrowed slightly. 'What do you mean? I came here to start my business.'

'Yes, but . . . why Chatternwell? How did you choose this town? Are you from Wiltshire?'

A touch of colour rose in her cheeks. William noted it with interest.

'I am originally from Somerset. My man of business searched for a good location to open a fashionable shop, but I wished for it to be in a smaller town with a strong community. Mr. Johnson did excellent research and found this location while I apprenticed with Signora Ricci in London, learning to manage a millinery and dress-rooms of quality.'

He tilted his head. 'You did not want to set up in London? Similar to . . . Signora Ricci?'

She shook her head. 'No. I have no family left, and I miss the time I worked at Baydon Hall. There was a strong sense of community amongst the servants, and I enjoyed the support we provided each other. Chatternwell is a good town. The people are productive, the town is doing well, and one can build professional relationships with honest proprietors.' Her voice softened. 'London is too large and aloof for the likes of me. I . . . like it here. It feels more like a home.'

William leaned back against the cushions and turned his gaze up to the dark beams of the ceiling, thoughtful.

He had grown up in Chatternwell. Worked here as a boy, then as a man. Other than his years fighting Boney, he had known no other home. He had never thought about the town in such deliberate terms. It had simply been the place of his birth, the place to which he had returned.

Now, hearing his home described by someone who had chosen it — who had seen its strengths and its promise — was strangely affecting. It made him view the cobbled streets and ageing cottages with fresh eyes.

As he drifted into a light doze, her words nestled into his mind. For better or worse, Chatternwell was his home.

* * *

William sat in the back of the local church, in the very last pew. It was nearest the door, so it would allow him to leave quickly after the service. In other words, he could reduce how many of his neighbours he would need to engage with. When they visited him in his smithy, he could feign politeness for the sake of business. But after a church service, people were more garrulous. Friendly. They invited him to their homes for Sunday dinners. If he left in haste, he would offend fewer of the townsfolk and be able to return to his smithy to work without interference.

Although this could have been any given Sunday, William realised in a vague sense that he was dreaming, because his ankle was miraculously healed. The last thing he could recall was falling asleep in his front room, and the soft sound of Caroline breathing deeply as she slumbered.

He tilted his head in an attempt to hear the vicar's words. For some reason, they were garbled, as if coming from a great distance, but he could just make out the word manger. This must be the Christmas service! If he had not injured himself, he would have attended this very day.

The vicar droned on, William scarcely able to hear any of it from the back of the church. He stood dutifully and sang hymns, sitting back down but prepared to run for the door as soon as he possibly could. Glancing up at the windows high behind him, William noted that the sky was overcast and it was snowing lightly.

Rustling in the pews ahead of him brought his attention back to the altar. People dressed in their Sunday best were beginning to stand, chattering to each other. The service must be over! Springing to his feet, he made for the exit, jamming his hat on his head as he opened the door to stride out into the wintry landscape beyond.

'Mr. Jackson!'

The voice was directly behind him — he could not pretend he did not hear. He continued to walk on, but threw a glance over his shoulder. 'Dr. Hadley, how are you this fine Christmas Day?'

The doctor nearly ran to keep pace with

him as William's longer legs ate up the distance down the path to the roadway. 'I am well, Mr. Jackson. It is good to see you in fine health, sir!'

William threw a smile at the older man. He did not wish to offend Dr. Hadley, who he had to admit was a good sort. The doctor had taken care of the townspeople for decades, accepting trade when they had not the means to pay. William reached the road and started towards Market Street, his boots crunching on freshly fallen snow as the doctor hurried to keep up with him.

William would relent his pace, but if he did, then more of his neighbours would engage him in conversation, and he wanted to build the new lock he had been thinking of. If it worked, the device could make him a fortune. Perhaps allow him to sell the smithy and live on its proceeds.

Beside him, Dr. Hadley was huffing in his effort to keep up. 'Mr. Jackson, I would be remiss if I did . . . not invite you to our Christmas feast . . . I promised Mrs. Hadley I would!'

William halted. They were some distance

from the church, and most of the parish was still inside. 'That is very kind of you, Dr. Hadley. Tell your wife thank you, and bid her all the best wishes for the holiday season.' He knew the doctor was merely being polite by extending the invitation. They had no true bonds between them. William had cultivated no friendships since his return from the war. These people would barely notice if he left town.

Dr. Hadley's face fell, his hat tilting to one side in his dejection before he reached up to straighten it. 'You will not attend?'

'I would love to taste Mrs. Hadley's Christmas pudding, but I am afraid I am otherwise committed. Please, enjoy your feast and do not concern yourself with me. You have other guests to attend, I am certain.'

'Yes, but . . .'

William gestured back to the churchyard before doffing his hat. 'Your wife is looking for you. Season's greetings, doctor.'

When Dr. Hadley turned to locate his wife, William took the opportunity to walk away and turn in to Market Street.

Soon he was in his smithy, wearing his

leather apron and studying a page covered in pencil drawings. He needed to heat the coal in his forge, and he could begin his work on the lock. He could, of course, have worked on this any day, but he had planned to work during the solitude of the holidays to keep his memories at bay.

Just as he placed the graphite pencil down on the counter, the sound of humming began in the distance. Slowly, the humming grew in volume, and William realised he was to receive a visitor at the moment that the smithy door clicked and swung open. He knew who it would be before she came into view, but, nevertheless, he was startled by her entrance when she appeared.

Her hair was glowing, lit from behind by weak sunlight, and she wore the frivolous cloak with the fur-lined cuffs that fell to the floor. She looked like an angel sent from heaven to scold him for working on this blessed day, but her expression was benign, and she smiled gently when she caught sight of him.

'Fear not,' said he, for mighty dread

had seized their troubled mind;
'glad tidings of great joy I bring
to you and all mankind.'

It was eerie, her staring directly into his eyes as she sang the verse.

He stepped back, his eyes widening with irrational fear at what she was to show him this time. She walked in, shutting the door and approaching him at the counter. With hazel eyes twinkling, she gazed up at him and asked, 'Why are you working on Christmas Day, William?'

'I . . . that is . . . there is no one for me to spend it with.' As he said the words, he wondered if it was true in light of Caroline's appearance once more in his dreams. Revelations from the earlier nightmare had proved that his philosophy about tamping down his emotions had been an error. Was she to reveal another aspect of his life to question?

Caroline held out her hand. Once again, it was clean, delicate, and perfect. His own were covered in soot from drawing near the forge, and he was certain he bore smudges on his cheeks and forehead, but there was no point in balking. He held out his dirty paw to clasp it.

'Chatternwell is a good town filled with good people.'

'Yes, I do not argue that point, but — '

'Close your eyes.'

William obeyed, shutting his eyes with the knowledge that it was futile to fight whatever was to come. The quiet of the smithy disappeared into a melee of merriment, and he could hear Dr. Hadley. Opening his eyes, he found that he and Caroline now stood in a dining room observing a Christmas feast.

Dr. Hadley sat at the head of the table, with his sons and their wives. Mrs. Hadley sat to his left, instead of the customary distance at the foot of the table. She was dressed in a fine velvet gown, with a lacy fichu draping her décolletage and matching the mobcap adorning her fair hair.

Through the door, William could see a second table in the hall where children sat eating their Christmas pie.

The tables were laden with plates, serving dishes, and gleaming silver. Wine had been poured, and a large Christmas goose had been carved. Hadley's eldest son finished telling an anecdote, and both men and women burst into laughter.

Caroline squeezed his hand and nodded her head to Dr. Hadley and his wife. They had their heads bent together, and Caroline drew him forward so he could hear what they were saying.

'You invited the blacksmith, and he declined?'

'Yes, Martha. I practically chased him down the street to deliver the invitation.'

Martha was a cheerful, buxom woman who took part in charitable works about town. Her blonde hair was now streaked with grey, but her blue eyes were still lively with humour and intelligence. She had been a friend of William's mother, who had died when he was a boy, and she had always made a point of seeking him out to ask after his well-being. Shame at his lack of interest in the generous woman suddenly presented itself, to William's dismay.

'I worry over little William.' William nearly snorted — he was twice the size of

Mrs. Hadley. 'He has not been the same since he returned from the war. I fear his mother would be most disappointed in me for allowing such aloofness to develop in her sweet boy. It is high time he finds himself a wife. A friend. Anyone.'

'I quite agree. But what am I to do? Every holiday I invite him to join us, and every holiday he declines.'

Martha peered over her shoulder towards her grandchildren, who were eating the feast with gusto, smiles on their little faces as they chattered together. 'I just wish he could experience the joy of family. He was such a happy boy before he left to fight Boney. He never smiles anymore. It quite distresses me to think of the change in him. William is a good man.'

Dr. Hadley nodded. 'That he is. He runs an honest business and has created work for our men and boys.'

William turned away. Why was Caroline doing this? He had finally rediscovered his living essence, but now he was to be confronted with the consequences of his self-imposed isolation. He tried to pull his hand from her clasp, but she would not let him. She broke off from her low humming.

'Close your eyes, William.'

He did so emphatically, not wanting to hear the rest of the conversation, nor to ponder his inadequacies. Inadequacies such as being alone today while Dr. Hadley enjoyed a feast with loved ones. The doctor was building a veritable legacy with the sheer number of family and the seasonal elation to be found in this home.

William thought they would return to the smithy, but the sound of festive merriment was replaced by a crackling fire blended with the distant sound of waves crashing on rocks. His eyes flew open to discover Uncle Albert and Aunt Gertrude sitting at their dining room table with a small feast laid out. A third place had been set, but there was no evidence of a guest.

Just as before, Aunt Gertrude appeared sad. She had appeared sad since learning of the death of Charles, her only child. William had not seen her cheery in some years.

'I had hoped that this year he would come. He is all we have left.'

Uncle Albert exhaled deeply. 'Perhaps it was a mistake to leave Chatternwell.'

Aunt Gertrude nodded. 'It was. William has not been the same since . . .' She struggled to a halt. 'We should have stayed for his sake. Do you think . . . he knows we love him?'

'I do not know, dear. You told him he was invited, I presume?'

'Every holiday. I told him there is always a place laid for him, if he ever changes his mind and finds the time to join us. I . . . I just want him to be happy again.'

William was stricken. He did not mean to cause his last remaining family any more pain than he already had.

Once again, he felt his eyes moisten, admitting to himself that his conduct had been selfish. He had not stopped to think that his beloved aunt might need him, that he had a responsibility. His life had been spared, while Charles had sacrificed his. It was William's duty to be there for his relations, to bring them some peace and not to be a cause of concern.

It was hard to stomach that his uncle and

aunt had retired to Cornwall three years earlier, and William had yet to visit them.

Turning to Caroline, he pulled her firmly around by the hand so she stood in front of him.

'Why are you doing this?' he demanded.

'No man can live alone, William. You must cherish the support of your friends. You must cherish the family you have left. You must accept that they are there for you, and you are there for them. You deserve to be loved.'

William shook his head. He had not meant to cause any pain.

This dream had left him with more questions than answers.

* * *

His ankle was throbbing when William woke up. To his surprise, the clock on the mantelpiece proclaimed it was only eleven o'clock. This was turning out to be a very strange evening.

Near him, Caroline gave a little snort in her sleep and then, slowly, her eyes opened. Noticing he was awake, she sat up, throwing her blanket aside to swing her feet down to the floor. 'Are you in need of something? Tea? Privacy for . . .' Caroline gestured to where the chamber pot rested under the settee.

'No, just your company.'

Caroline used both hands to smooth her hair and then straighten her wrap. 'Oh.'

'I was thinking about what you said. How Chatternwell is a good town, filled with good people.'

She nodded, reaching over to take up her neglected cup and sip on its cold contents. 'It is.'

'It made me realise I have not appreciated what I have the way I should.'

The corner of Caroline's mouth quirked up in a crooked smile. 'You failed to count your blessings?'

'I did. It must be hard for you.'

She frowned in confusion. 'What do you mean?'

'You said you have no family. I am afraid I have not appreciated that I do.

I cannot imagine being entirely alone, with not one relation left.'

Caroline's eyes flittered away. 'It . . . is difficult,' she finally admitted in a thick voice.

'You have no one?'

William felt a pang when he noticed that her eyes now glittered and suspected that he had drawn tears to her eyes. What a bleak holiday they were sharing.

'I had some friends . . . but I made a horrible mistake and lost them. I have learned to be self-reliant.'

'And count your blessings?'

She chuckled, and William observed a flash of her usual optimism return. 'And count my blessings.'

'What blessings do you count tonight, Caroline?'

She inhaled a deep breath and thought.

'I have my own shop. I live in a lovely town and work with wonderful women. I must be viewed favourably because the doctor entrusted you to my care. I was to spend Christmas alone, but instead I am spending it . . . with you.'

He could build a better future, allow for closer connections than he had these last few years. Appreciate the community he lived in and allow some emotions back into his life. This evening had changed him for the better, and he looked forward to the days ahead, now that he had time to think about the revelations of the evening. It was high time he took some time to visit his uncle and aunt at their seaside cottage. As soon as his injury improved, he would do so.

Caroline shifted and sat on the table. She felt his leg with gentle fingers.

'I am going to apply a fresh poultice. Would you like anything?'

'Warm water and cloths? Perhaps you could collect my nightshirt?'

'You would like to wash up?'

He nodded. 'I was working in this shirt all day.'

Caroline made a sound of assent, taking up things from the table and leaving for the kitchen. Soon she returned with the bowl of warm water and cloths, laying them out on the table. Once she left the room, he pulled his shirt off and took up one of the cloths to bathe himself.

The fresh, clean water was refreshing, and he felt considerably more comfortable when she came back in with his nightshirt, careful to avert her eyes from his bare torso as she handed it over.

Quickly, she cleared the table once more, and he could hear her tidying up in the kitchen while he pulled his nightshirt on. Leaving his buckskins on, he straightened up the settee pillows to settle back into a reclining position. This brief interlude of domestic bliss was a pleasant change in routine, especially given the time of the year. He was fortunate the doctor had found such an excellent companion to nurse him back to health. Spending the night with the wrong person would have been torturous, and Caroline's presence had brought a much-needed reprieve from his bad dreams. For the first time in years, he had slept without dreaming of war and bloodshed — a minor miracle in itself.

All in all, this Christmas Eve had been

something of a success despite the swollen, bruised appendage.

Caroline returned to apply a fresh poultice, quietly affixing it to his leg with a bandage. Then she cleared the room and once again could be heard moving around the kitchen.

William drifted off to sleep in the darkened room, his body fatigued as he gradually slipped back into another dream.

6

The Future

Early morning, Christmas Day (The First Day of Christmas)

The sky was overcast — brooding and grim. Market Street was covered in a fresh fall of snow. The world was silent, muffled by the clouds overhead and flakes blanketing the roadway. William looked about and realised it must still be Christmas Day, the shops sporting festive Christmas boughs in their darkened windows. Across the street was the empty post office, the interior dark and deserted. If that was the post office, he must be standing in front of Caroline's shop.

He turned to look, noting a fresh display of ribbons through the window, along with festive sprigs and boughs draping the windows and counters.

Why was he back on this day? Was there some new revelation to uncover?

Not knowing what came next, William

walked towards his cottage. As he approached a cross street, Dr. Hadley appeared, walking from the direction of the church.

'Mr. Jackson! Season's greetings to you!' The doctor paused to meet him at the corner.

William realised something was not right. Dr. Hadley's hair was whiter. His thick moustache was also white, and he had far more lines on his face. He appeared to have aged several years.

William rubbed his face, confused by this turn of events. Was this a future Christmas?

'The same to you and Mrs. Hadley, doctor.'

'Thank you, Mr. Jackson. I must be on my way, but I do not need to tell you! You have a full house waiting for you!'

The doctor was not going to invite him to his Christmas feast as he did each year? And what did he mean . . . a full house? While William pondered their conversation, the doctor had walked off in the direction of his home. He shook his head, not sure what to make of this new situation.

Shrugging, he resumed his walk home, feeling rather bleak and lonely. It would be lovely if Caroline showed up to guide him somewhere, the world eerily quiet as the snow began to fall once more.

An eternity later — the walk seeming to take much longer than usual — he reached his front door, where he stood hesitantly. All was quiet, and he was reluctant to enter his empty home and spend Christmas alone yet again. He wanted to embrace life, reconnect with his neighbours and family. Perhaps even visit Caroline in her millinery and converse with her while she worked — not enter his cold, silent cottage.

From behind the front door, he heard humming with a surge of pleasure. She was coming! They would accompany each other, and she would reveal some new way to improve his lot. It was a sweet delight to hear her melodic voice break into song.

'All glory be to God on high,
and to the earth be peace;
to those on whom his favor rests
goodwill shall never cease.'

The sound grew closer until, finally, the

lock clicked, and his front door swung open.

'William, there you are! We have been waiting to serve dinner!'

He blinked. Was she not going to ask him some peculiarly discerning question as she had before?

Caroline reached out a hand, and he looked down. This time she wore gloves, as if she were cold. Shaking his head in confusion, he looked down at his own hand to discover that he, too, was wearing gloves. At least this time, he saw no evidence of his hand being soiled as in the earlier dreams. He reached out and clasped her hand with confidence as she smiled and drew him closer.

Then, to his surprise, she bobbed up on her toes to plant a kiss on his cheek. Granted, it landed low in his beard because of their disparity in height, but it was welcome nonetheless.

Caroline turned and pulled him along to guide him inside, William shutting out the cold to discover that the cottage was warm with ambient heat. The fires must be lit.

As he looked about the sitting room, he was startled to find Uncle Albert sitting at a table beside a young boy with almost black hair. They were studying a diagram sketched with a graphite pencil, their heads bowed together. William noticed the room had been redecorated. Above the fireplace hung a painting of Chatternwell at dawn, painted from one of the rolling hills. Depicted there was the church spire, and chimneys puffing cheerful smoke. The rug had been replaced with one of oranges and purples to pick out the colours of the painting, along with the cushions on the settees. New curtains hung in the windows, and the walls were painted in claret.

'Charles, do you wish to greet your papa?' Caroline called across the room.

William's head whipped in her direction to confirm she was addressing the boy directly.

Were they not spectators of this scene, then? Were they active participants?

Looking back at the table, he saw the young boy raise his head. Blazing blue eyes found him standing there, and the child hopped down from his chair to race across the room and throw his little arms around

William's thighs. 'Papa! You are home!'

William blinked several times, finally raising a hand to the boy's shoulder to give him a hesitant pat.

Uncle Albert approached with a broad grin. 'William, I have been teaching your boy about locks. I showed him the one you invented.' He indicated the table with a wave of his hand.

William was speechless, only able to nod mutely as he took in his uncle's cheerful demeanour. He had not seen Uncle Albert this happy in years.

Caroline dropped to her haunches. 'Are you ready for dinner, Charles? Or do you need to wash your hands?'

The boy, no more than seven years of age, grinned with an impish twinkle in his intense blue eyes. 'I must wash up,' he confessed, then ran through the door to the kitchen. Caroline pulled William by the hand and followed the boy. Entering the back room, William found Aunt Gertrude holding a small girl on her hip, tendrils of greying hair having escaped the neat little bun at her nape. It amazed him to see his aunt with a huge smile as she used a cloth to wipe the child's fingers, which were red with the juice of cranberries. 'Now, Margaret, look what a mess you have made!'

'Aunt Gertrude?'

His aunt turned to smile broadly in greeting. 'William, you are home! Dinner is almost ready, lad.'

William had not seen his aunt in such fine spirits for years, not since before he had broken the bad news about her son. Yet, here she stood with colour in her cheeks and her eyes glistening with joy. His chest expanded with elation at seeing her in such good spirits. The little girl in his aunt's arms looked about with wide, inquisitive eyes.

Noticing William, her cherubic face lit up. 'Papa!' she squealed, wiggling with excitement to ignite a yearning.

He swallowed hard, looking carefully at the two children. Noting the boy bore a resemblance to himself, while the tiny girl wrapped in Aunt Gertrude's arm had blonde hair and lively hazel eyes. This was Caroline's daughter. His daughter?

On the table was the evidence of a dinner

in its finishing stages, and the smell of roasted meat caused a rumble in his belly. The entire room was filled with domestic bliss and festive spirits, sprigs of holly adorning the windows, and William felt true happiness standing in his kitchen surrounded by the ones he loved.

Turning to Caroline, pulling on her hand to get her attention, he questioned her earnestly. 'What is this?'

She gazed at him with a warm expression before responding, 'This is the future, William. If you allow it.'

William was overcome, his throat growing thick with the sheer emotion enveloping him as he took in the sight of his uncle and aunt restored to good spirits. New life that had been brought into the world and set things right, with two healthy children to build the future.

Turning, he pulled Caroline into an embrace. He wanted this! All of this. He wanted children and hope. He wanted reconciliation and good cheer. He wanted her!

As he engulfed her with his arms, feeling her slight body against his own, she giggled. 'Careful, William. Do not squish our babe.'

Which was when he felt the roundness of her belly pressed against him. Caroline was increasing, and with this news, he nearly wept his joy into her vanilla-scented hair.

'Merry Christmas, sunshine,' he whispered, feeling her lips curve into a smile against his neck.

'Merry Christmas, blacksmith.'

* * *

She was half asleep, dozing on the shorter settee and wishing she could stretch out properly on a bed, when Caroline heard the blacksmith mumbling in his sleep.

She could not make out the rest of the words, but she could pick out one.

'. . . sunshine . . .'

What on earth could the blacksmith be dreaming about?

She dug an elbow into the settee cushion and raised her head to peer across to where he lay.

'. . . Christmas . . .'

Caroline tried to see his expression in the dim light of the fading fire. Was he in distress? Should she wake him once more?

'... Caroline...

She bit her lip. He was dreaming of her!

One of Chatternwell's most eligible men was currently prone across the room and dreaming of silly little Caroline of Somerset. An orphan and an unchaste woman of few redeeming traits!

What a bizarre situation this was proving to be. There was nothing to compare this night to — no similar experience to call upon. She did not know what to make of the strange events that had unfolded these past hours.

In a day or so, she would leave this cottage and return to the real world, outside of this strange interlude. When she and William met in the future, they would have to pretend this had never happened. In fact, they would have to return to their polite distance as Mrs. Brown and Mr. Jackson, their only commonality being that they each owned a business on Market Street. This entire evening would be swept away as if it had never happened.

The thought was unexpectedly desolate. She liked the blacksmith, especially since he had relaxed his grim mood and revealed some of his struggles.

Many women in this town coveted William for his handsome form and successful livelihood. Yet Caroline knew something else about him. She was the only woman in Chatternwell aware he had injured himself while secretly helping the old widow next door by repairing her roof on Christmas Eve.

He was an honourable man, and she had to admit their earlier conversation had been thrilling — when he had confessed that she had influenced his thoughts and lightened some undisclosed burden he had been carrying. The shift in his mood was palpable, and she was apparently the cause of it.

The thought of gathering her things to walk out the door was rather disheartening.

Work!

Caroline drew a deep breath, slightly mollified at the reminder of what would take the place of this increasingly intimate connection she was forming with William.

Work will keep your mind from wandering about!

She nodded to herself. Close relationships were not permitted. This was an aberration — a freak occurrence. Once this holiday was over, so too would be this strange bond they had formed over the course of the night. Work would distract her from any yearnings that might disturb her thoughts.

As she reached this conclusion, feeling better for having a plan to get past these unprecedented events, Caroline realised that William's eyes were open. He was staring at her with the oddest expression. Was it . . . admiration?

Caroline sat up. 'Do you need anything, William?'

He licked his lips to moisten them, then spoke in a low voice. 'Would you check my ankle?'

'Of course.' She swung her feet to the floor and bounced up, quickly navigating the room to light a candle before sitting on the low table. She pulled his blanket up to reveal his ankle in the low light, then gently felt around.

'It seems considerably less swollen. Shall I replace the poultice?'

William shook his head, reaching out a hand to take hold of the edge of her wrap. Caroline's mouth went dry as her gaze dropped to his powerful, bronzed hand. She noticed with fascination the dusting of black hair.

'You are a most extraordinary young woman, Miss Brown.'

His voice was husky, his gaze steady — so unwavering it stirred a flutter deep within her chest.

'I . . . am?' she croaked out, before swallowing hard, tension thrumming between them, their gazes locked.

'And very beautiful. The most beautiful woman I have ever beheld.'

Caroline swallowed hard again. 'That is not possible. What of Miss Jolie, the daughter of Sir Walter?'

His lips quirked in amusement. 'I am not well acquainted with Miss Jolie, but she has never turned my head. You, on the other hand, have refused to leave my thoughts since we met.'

At this revelation, Caroline blinked. 'You have been thinking . . . about me?'

'Aye,' was his only response as he continued to finger the wrap between his thumb and forefinger. Caroline was tempted to fall forward, only holding herself back by sheer force of will as she focused on his lips and relived their kiss from earlier that night. Her skin still tingled from the scrape of his beard.

William drew a deep breath, and then reluctantly released the fabric to drop his hand to the settee.

'You shall have to walk away now, sunshine.'

Crushing disappointment overcame her. Her lips formed words without thought. 'I am . . . not . . . an honourable woman.'

Her shameful whisper was as loud as

a shout, with no nocturnal sounds other than the crackling fire to disguise her words. Caroline clapped a hand over her mouth in dismay.

Why would you tell him that?

Distressed, she clapped her hand over her mouth once more, horrified that she had done it. Destroyed their burgeoning affection. She had wanted to prolong their shared intimacy, but her impulsive words had driven a permanent wedge between them. There had been a wish to share herself, but now her thoughtless declaration would cause him to lose his regard, and she would return to her isolation. If she was fortunate, he would keep her secret.

Caroline squeezed her eyes shut in regret. It had been so long since she had let her walls down to share a genuine experience with another person. There were so many excuses she could state for having done so now. It was the holidays. She was lonely. William was the first man to gaze at her with such blazing admiration.

None of it signified, because she had revealed her darkest secret to a veritable stranger, and now he would display his disdain, and she would be alone once more. Her throat tightened, and threatening tears burned.

Eventually, she realised she could no longer avoid his reaction, and her eyes flickered open. The blacksmith was watching her, contemplating her declaration. Caroline wished she could sink into the table and disappear until, what seemed an eternity later, he finally responded,

'Whatever regrets you harbour, I have done too much wrong in my life to judge you.'

His reply loosened the bands of despair wrapped around her chest as she finally sucked air into her burning lungs.

* * *

William had every intention of wooing the fascinating woman who sat by his side. After the glimpse of their possible future his dream had revealed, her fate was sealed. He was going to marry Caroline Brown and live in sunshine for the rest of his days.

However, he realised she had not shared the experiences of his dream, so his decision would seem abrupt. He had yet to convince her that they were fated to be together.

Sensing there was more to her declaration regarding her shame, William concluded he did not care what dark past she might be hiding. Whatever had prompted her to move to Chatternwell was irrelevant to his determination to entwine his future with hers.

He had seen into her heart, and the beauty of her spirit utterly beguiled him. She had brought him back from the dead with her talk of blessings, the value of friends and family, and finally with her views on the future.

There was no possibility, now that the light had cast away the shadows of his past, that he would relinquish her. All that remained was to lead her to a similar conclusion — that life would be meaningless without him at her side.

Then the vicar would read their vows, and Caroline would come to live in his home. She would change his life as she saw fit, and he would worship her from that day forward while they shared the joy of creating their own family together.

Somehow, he had to bring her to this decision with determined subtlety.

Since he had opened his eyes, he had been aware of her. Enthralled by her presence, he was compelled to draw her closer within his reach.

William noted how Caroline's gaze remained fastened to his. A flush touched her cheeks, and he caught the faint hitch of her breath. Could it be she was as captivated as he?

He drew a breath and took a chance, raising his hand to reach for her tentatively. Triumph swelled his chest when Caroline came willingly into his arms. Her hazel eyes were luminous in the dim firelight, and when her lips parted with a soft sigh, it was the only invitation he needed.

William wrapped an arm around her slight waist, drawing her close before cupping her face in his hands. He tilted her head back, brushing his mouth over hers with aching reverence, then deepened the kiss with fervent longing.

Caroline clutched the fabric of his shirt, her fingers curling as she drew closer, returning his kiss with quiet intensity. Her lips were soft, the moment lingering — tender, suffused with emotion. What stirred between them was not mere attraction; it was connection. It was hope. It felt like the first glimmer of something enduring and true. But did she sense it as well?

7
The Crescendo

Several minutes passed as she fought to recover her breath, seated at his side while she slowly descended from the heights of magical kisses. Eventually, she rose to tidy herself and pull her night rail back into place. Embarrassment was setting in.

What have I done?

She had kissed a man with unseemly enthusiasm. A man who was not her husband. Again.

A hand came up to rub the ache in her chest.

This served only to prove she was weak. An unchaste woman.

She handed William a clean cloth, unable to meet his eyes, before walking over to the other settee to retrieve her wrap. As she lifted the garment, she heard William settle back behind her.

'Join me?'

Caroline stared down at the embroidered fabric in her hand, uncertain how to respond or make sense of his request.

'Please?'

Tears sprang to her eyes. This was unprecedented. Did the blacksmith truly wish to hold her? Just hold her? She glanced towards him. His blue eyes were earnest in the low firelight, and as before, she saw admiration — perhaps even affection — shining in his gaze.

Without quite making the decision, she drifted closer. William shifted over, creating space and lifting an arm in invitation. Caroline did not know what to make of it, but the urge to settle beside him was impossible to resist. She lay down carefully, wrapping a slender arm across his chest.

The blacksmith tucked her head beneath his chin, his muscled arm curling around her in a gentle, protective embrace. After a few moments, it became clear he had fallen asleep, his breathing even and deep. Caroline listened to the steady thrum of his heart beneath her ear, the heat of his body seeping into hers, and felt astonishment.

William seemed to regard her with genuine esteem. Shame, which had burned so hotly, slowly began to dissipate.

She had broken her vow not to grow close to anyone. Caroline knew from past mistakes that she could not be trusted to protect what mattered most, but just for tonight, she would allow herself this fleeting reprieve. The blacksmith seemed to like her. More than that, he had seen something in her that others had not.

She would clutch this moment — however ephemeral — and hold it tightly until the world reclaimed them both.

Yes, she was weak. She had proven that. But for one night only, she wanted to forget her failings and accept the comfort of William's embrace. The slow rhythm of his heart, beating steadily beneath her cheek, lulled her towards sleep.

When she awakened, the room was dim with the hush of a winter morning. The candle had burned down, and the fire was no more than glowing embers. She stirred slightly, intending to rise, but William grumbled in his sleep and pulled her closer.

Caroline blinked rapidly in confusion.

Is this what it is like to be married to a kind man? To be cherished?

Work, Caroline! Do not get any ideas about love and companionship!

She lay perfectly still, scarcely daring to breathe. The notion was so very tempting. Yet the familiar mental refrain — work is safety — held no comfort this morning. She did not wish to return to reality. Not yet.

William smelt of leather and fire, of soap and metal. She nestled in closer, and this time, it was with intention. In the warmth of his arms, she felt — at last — safe.

When she awoke again, she found William pressing a kiss to the crown of her head. She looked up into his eyes, blue and steady, and he smiled at her — a soft, intimate smile that crinkled the corners of his eyes — before gently kissing her brow.

'I am afraid I need privacy,' he whispered.

Caroline immediately lifted her head. He slowly released his hold, and she sat up.

'Do you need any help?'

'A fresh poultice and water to clean up would be appreciated.'

She nodded and began clearing the table before slipping from the room, closing the door behind her so he could tend to himself. In the kitchen, she put water to boil and prepared a fresh cloth. Once the linens were cleaned and folded, she assembled a tea tray with sandwiches, fresh tea, and the new poultice.

When she called to confirm his readiness, she returned to find him seated upright, his long nightshirt neat and his dark beard softened by fresh stubble. His folded breeches rested on the table. He looked . . . wonderful. At ease. At home.

Caroline could not help but imagine what it might be like to see him thus each morning.

They shared a quiet breakfast, sipping tea and eating sandwiches. There was peace in the domestic stillness, a harmony that felt entirely unfamiliar and wholly comforting.

Once she had finished her meal, she leaned back and sighed. 'I shall clean up and then I must attend Christmas service. My absence would raise questions.'

'As will mine,' he muttered, reluctant.

'Yes, but eventually the town will know you were injured. My absence will lack a convincing explanation.'

William tilted his head in slow agreement. 'You should go.'

'I do not know how long it will last, but afterwards I shall pick up my order from Mr. Andrews and return to prepare your meal.'

'Thank you. For everything you have done.'

Caroline smiled, her cheeks warming. 'I am reluctant to leave. It is as though I have been dreaming, and now I must wake to find the world unchanged.'

William regarded her closely before

replying in a hoarse voice, 'It was no dream. Everything has changed.'

Her brow creased at that. He must realise that this interlude could not last. As much as she wished to linger in the fragile bloom of their kinship, life would intrude. And she had nothing of real value to offer a man such as William Jackson.

Despite his earlier kindness, he did not know the full truth. He did not know the weight of her betrayal, the damage she had caused. Not even her dearest friend had forgiven her.

The blacksmith would not either, if he knew.

She cleared her throat and stood. 'I shall clean up before I leave for the servicc.'

* * *

William lay back, a book resting on his chest, his gaze fixed on the dark beams overhead. Since Caroline had left through the back door, an eerie hush had settled over the cottage. It felt as though he had slipped into one of the dreams from the night before, the quiet only broken by the faint crackle of the fire. A dream without her.

He regretted the sequence of events.

Caroline was to be his wife. Of that, he was certain. But his desire for her — his need to feel her near — had overtaken him in the small hours, and now all was uncertain. The line between what had passed between them and what ought to have passed had blurred, and he could not be sure where they now stood.

He ought to have courted her properly. That would have been the sensible course. Respectful. Safe. But last night had not been a time for sensibility. It had been magic. He had been caught in the power of their connection, swept along by the beauty of her spirit and the warmth of her presence, and for a brief moment, he had lost all sense but that she belonged beside him.

He only hoped his moment of foolishness would not thwart his intentions.

It weighed on him — that Caroline was hiding something. Some secret that burdened her spirit. Whatever it was, she had not realised that nothing — nothing — she might confess could alter his regard for her. The shame she carried was invisible to him. He saw only a courageous, remarkable woman. But now, in the silence of his sitting room, with her gone, doubt crept in. The future he had dreamed of so clearly seemed suddenly delicate, as if it might fracture with the slightest misstep.

He must convince her. Today. Before she left for good to return to her rooms, to the world they both knew so well. Their connection felt inseparable from the spirit of the holiday. A fragile enchantment. And if they parted without an understanding, he feared that spell might not be so easily recaptured.

William sighed and shut his eyes.

The vicar. Blast the man. He had better not keep the parish locked in the pews until sundown, rambling through his fifth point on humility or his annual treatise on the mystery of the Virgin birth. Reverend Murton was an earnest man, but he often forgot that sermons had a natural conclusion — and that not everyone in the village was so patient.

William needed the time. He needed to speak with Caroline again before the sun went down on this strange and wonderful Christmas Day. Before the spell of their night together dissolved into memory and regret. He had seen a glimpse of a future filled with laughter and children and love — and he intended to make it so.

* * *

Caroline shifted upon her rented pew — one of the privileges afforded by her increased income was that she no longer had to stand through the entire church service. The vicar delivered a lengthy sermon from his pulpit, but she scarcely heard a word. Could there be a more uncomfortable place to reflect upon one's transgressions than here, in the holiest of places?

At least she could be thankful that it was a Christmas service of goodwill, rather than a discourse upon the evils of mankind. Rising to sing a hymn, her eyes fixed dutifully upon the words in her book, Caroline tried to make sense of her choices. Her lips moved to form the lines of the verse, but her thoughts remained far from the music.

This connection with William differed from her experience with the earl. She knew it — *knew it* — but that did not erase the reality of her past. Two years earlier, she had betrayed her dearest friend in the most shameful manner a woman could.

It was one thing to be unwise with a man. It was quite another to break the sacred bonds of friendship. The deeper scar had been the loss of her place — her family — at Baydon Hall. Annie Greer had grown up without a father, but at least her position had been secure. Caroline had forfeited hers, and she had only herself to blame.

As the hymn drew to a close and the congregation resumed their seats — save for the poorer townsfolk who remained standing at the back — Caroline fixed her gaze upon the stained-glass windows.

The root of her vow was not chastity. It was loyalty. It was the agony of having lost not merely a position, but a family. Miss Annabel, Mrs. Harris, the other servants — they had been her only true kin, once her parents and grandmother were gone. And she had thrown it all away for the charming smile of a nobleman.

That Miss Annabel had provided a reference had only deepened the wound. Caroline had not deserved such grace. She could not risk forming another bond she might one day break. She could not survive such a loss again. And yet — now that she was no longer in William's presence — she feared she had already grown too close.

She longed to return to him. To be with someone — anyone — who had looked upon her with something like affection.

The shame remained, but so too did the memory of warmth. A single day in good company — might she not be permitted that?

What had become of her tidy plans? Her resolute focus on work? Simplicity had been her shield, but she had let it fall. She had allowed her emotions to awaken, and now there was no pretending she was unaffected.

As the congregation rose for the final hymn, Caroline pushed her troubled musings aside. This was not the hour to dwell upon disappointment. Tomorrow would come soon enough. For today, she would share a Christmas meal with William Jackson, and she would cherish each moment. She would hold fast to this last memory of comfort before returning to the quiet life she had made for herself.

The final chords faded, and Caroline blinked, startled to realise the service had ended. Parishioners stood in conversation, dressed in their Sunday best and exchanging warm wishes. She rose and stepped into the aisle just as a familiar voice called out.

'Merry Christmas, Mrs. Brown!'

Annie Greer beamed up at her, her cheeks rosy with good health.

Caroline smiled, touched by the girl's vivacity. 'Merry Christmas, Annie!'

'Did you enjoy the service?'

Caroline hesitated. 'I did.' It was the truth — or near enough. 'Are you going to collect your goose from Mr. Andrews?'

'Yes, Mama and I shall leave shortly.' Annie turned to wave at her mother, who stood talking with another widow. Mrs. Greer waved cheerfully at Caroline, her face flushed with vitality. She looked stronger — healthier — than she had in weeks.

Caroline's chest swelled. She had done this. She had helped. That was something.

Bidding Annie goodbye, she moved ahead of the crowd, her pace brisk as she made for Market Street. At the baker's, she knocked smartly, and Mr. Andrews opened the door. She had paid earlier in the week, so it took but a moment to collect her order.

Then she hurried back to her shop, entering the front so that any passer-by might witness her respectable arrival. Only once inside did she slip out the back and into the alley, her pulse quickening.

A sharp wind stole beneath the cuffs of her green velvet cloak, and Caroline laughed quietly to herself. William had been right — it was woefully ill-suited to winter weather — but she adored it. The cloak was feminine, luxurious, and entirely hers.

Reaching the cross street, she checked both directions. All was clear.

Lifting her skirts, she dashed across, her heart racing not only from the cold but from anticipation.

She wanted to see him. She wanted this moment. Just a little longer.

* * *

William's spirits lifted the instant he heard the back door swing open. He struggled into a seated position, hope blooming in his chest. Moments later, Caroline appeared, her cheeks flushed with delightful colour and her eyes alight with excitement.

'I have returned!'

'I have waited with bated breath.'

She beamed at him, and William inhaled deeply, exhilarated. It seemed his courtship had truly begun. Today, he would pursue the magnificent modiste who had stolen his heart.

'I find it absurd,' she teased, 'that the man who repairs locks for a living has one that clearly needs replacing.'

William laughed. 'Alas, I never find the time to repair my own home. I am always occupied with work. Though a modiste,' he added, gesturing to her cloak, 'should know how to fashion garments that do not freeze the wearer in winter.'

Caroline giggled. 'I shall prepare our meal. How is your ankle?'

'The swelling is down considerably. It

only pains me if I move too quickly. Perhaps it is not as badly sprained as it first appeared. Or your poultices are particularly effective.'

She smiled. 'I am so glad. You shall be back at your forge in no time. It must weary you to lie about.'

William beckoned her closer and took her delicate hand in his. Staring into her eyes, he murmured, 'Not when you are here.'

She bit her lip before smiling again. 'I ought to prepare our meal.'

Reluctantly, he let her hand go. 'Be quick,' he implored.

With a nod, she disappeared into the kitchen. William lay back with a contented sigh, whistling the tune of the carol Caroline had sung in his dreams. Once they were wed, she would always be within reach. They would share evenings by the fire, advise one another on their respective trades, and one day, God willing, raise flaxen-haired daughters with hazel eyes who would giggle beneath Christmas boughs.

He breathed deeply, awash with contentment. It must be the magic of the season. Or, perhaps, the magic of her.

When Caroline returned with a tray laden with food, he swung his legs down. 'I feel ashamed to watch you toil while I lie about like a lazy lout.'

She giggled, setting the tray down. 'Word about town is that you ought to lie about more often. I hear you work far too many hours.'

'I was filling my days. Too many thoughts I wished to avoid.'

She froze. 'You work to avoid your thoughts?'

'I did. But now I plan to turn over a new leaf.'

'Why?'

'Why change?'

She nodded.

William exhaled and rubbed at his beard. 'I had a younger cousin. My uncle — the blacksmith before me — was his father.'

'Had?'

He nodded. 'Charles and I went to

fight Napoleon together.'

'He died?'

'He did. His parents were devastated.'

'And you? How did you feel?'

William huffed. Of course she would ask the very question he avoided. 'He was my closest friend. And I watched him die.'

Caroline was quiet, her lip caught between her teeth. Then she crossed to sit beside him and placed her delicate hand over his.

'I am sorry.'

'You have brought me more comfort than you could possibly comprehend.'

'Me?'

'Every night since his death, I have dreamed of Charles. But last night . . . when you told me to count my blessings . . . the dream changed. I saw his sacrifice not as a loss, but a gift. I realised that by focusing on grief, I had failed to honour him. I must live — for the both of us.'

She looked down at their clasped hands.

'You are a good man, William. You deserve to live a full life.'

He released her hand only so he could pull her into his arms. Breathing in the familiar vanilla and peppermint of her hair, he murmured, 'What have you brought us to eat?'

She chuckled. 'Roast chicken. And a Christmas mince pie from Mr. Andrews.'

'What? No Christmas pudding?'

She laughed. 'I had no time to prepare one back in November.'

He groaned in exaggerated dismay. When she pulled back, he winked. 'We shall make do, I suppose.'

She smiled and handed him a plate laden with food. 'To make matters worse, we must eat on the settee.'

Taking a bite of the pie, William shut his eyes in bliss. 'Mr. Andrews is a marvel.'

Caroline hummed her agreement, the familiar melody sparking warmth in his chest. How strange that his soul could know hers so deeply — first in dreams, now in daylight. She had unlocked him, freed him.

And he wanted nothing more than to unlock her — to uncover every secret she held close.

He set his plate aside, then reached for hers and placed it with his. She blinked in surprise. Without a word, William slowly lowered himself onto one knee. Caroline gasped, her eyes wide as he took her hand in his.

'Caroline Brown,' he said softly, 'will you do me the honour of becoming my wife?'

8

The Argument

'Have you gone mad?' Her question was sincere. She was genuinely concerned the blacksmith had taken leave of his senses. 'You barely know me!'

'I know everything that matters,' he replied, his blue eyes earnest as he cradled her hand in his own. His fingers were rough, his palms calloused — a reminder of the work he did — bending iron to his will, shaping raw metal into useful tools. He was a builder. A craftsman. Steady, reliable.

And he was offering to marry her?

'Is this because we kissed?' she asked. 'You need not feel obligated. I knew what I was doing. I had no expectations of you.'

William chuckled. 'Nay, Caroline. You are a fine woman, and had that been the reason, I would still be honour-bound to do right by you. But the truth is . . . I had already decided on this course before we kissed so thoroughly.'

'What?'

'I had already made the decision to make you my wife.'

Her mind was swimming — a maelstrom of confusion and disbelief. No man had ever proposed to her before — certainly not one as respectable, admired, and sound of mind as William Jackson. She had imagined what it might be like to marry him, in the safety of secret dreams, but never had she believed he might desire it.

'You do not know me.'

'I know what matters,' he repeated gently. 'You are an admirable woman, and it would be my great honour to wed you.'

Her heart seized.

But he did not know her. Not truly. He did not know what she had done. Why she had come to Chatternwell. He did not know that her benefactor was Lord Saunton, who had paid for her shop and sent his man of business to arrange it all.

He did not know why Lord Saunton had done those things — or what Caroline had done to Miss Annabel to prompt them.

She could never share those truths. Not with William.

His regard had made her feel whole again, if only briefly. If she told him the truth, he would be disgusted — and it would sever the fragile bond between them. Better to carry the memory than to destroy what they had built in a single evening.

William must have sensed the shift in her, for he gave her hand a tender squeeze. 'I apologise for springing this on you. I had intended to court you properly, to coax you into accepting me . . . but I was overcome by the joy of sharing this day with you. I want it to never end. And I make no decisions lightly, Caroline.'

Her free hand rose to her cheeks, only to discover they were wet. Tears streamed down her face, unchecked and uncontrollable. She was flattered. Tempted. And terrified.

'What is it, sunshine?' William's voice was soft with concern.

'Could we not talk about this now?' Her voice cracked. She had looked forward to the final hours of Christmas with him. If she turned him down now — there was no other option — it would end the fragile peace they had found far too abruptly.

Her eyes were so filled with tears, she could barely see him.

He reached for a handkerchief and gently dabbed her cheeks. 'Is it so upsetting to contemplate a future with me?'

She shook her head. 'It is upsetting to contemplate a future without you.'

William released a deep breath, his shoulders lifting with the effort. 'Then let us set it aside for now. I am sorry to have interrupted our meal. Just . . . know that the offer stands.'

She nodded, tension easing as he awkwardly shifted himself back onto the settee. Caroline reached for her plate, but her thoughts remained with him — his words, his expression, his unwavering regard. She imagined what it might be like to say yes. To share dinners with him forevermore. To bear his children and teach her daughters to sew. To hand her child a silken strand of embroidery floss for the first time.

She imagined a little boy with William's dark hair and brilliant blue eyes, tugging the bellows chain with a determined little arm whilst his father held him aloft. It was so tempting.

If only she had not ruined her future two years ago — if only she had not broken her own trust in herself.

There could be no idyllic future for a woman who harboured such shameful secrets. No trust given to one who could not trust herself. Resolutely, she lifted her fork and took a bite of mince pie, forcing herself to focus on its sweetness. On this meal. On this moment.

These were dreams, nothing more. And they would have to sustain her.

* * *

As they ate in silence, William fought his frustration. He almost missed the emptiness of his soul these past years. At least then he had been entirely logical, not driven by impulse or unruly emotion. The success of his business had been built upon single-minded focus, yet he could scarcely recall what that had felt like since Caroline had awakened him from his self-imposed slumber and unravelled all his careful plans to remain indifferent.

His timing had been abysmal.

He was desperate to keep her at his side, to hold on to this unexpected magic between them. As the hour of her departure drew closer, the rising panic threatened to unman him.

He knew she harboured a secret, and it had been a grievous miscalculation to ignore the instinct that warned him of it. Proposing while she carried that invisible weight — whatever it was — had been foolish. All he could do now was try to restore her good cheer, distract her, and bide his time.

He would try again. Later.

Chewing slowly on the delicious mince pie, William forced himself to release the turmoil. If this was all he would have of her, then he would relish it. Every second.

'This is the first Christmas I have celebrated in some years,' he finally said, once his disappointment had dulled to something tolerable.

Caroline took a sip of her tea before replying, 'Because of what happened to your cousin?'

He nodded. 'I am pleased to be sharing this day with you.'

Her full lips curved into a gentle smile, and the sight eased something tight within him. Witnessing her weep earlier had undone him completely.

'As am I.'

He smiled in return. 'Last year, I worked after the Christmas service.'

She giggled. 'So did I! I was the housekeeper for a doctor in Somerset. We had to see to the household, and then we celebrated the following day with the Feast of Saint Stephen.'

'Yet here we are,' he murmured, 'together in Chatternwell, eating Mr. Andrews's pie.'

'Here we are,' she echoed softly.

William hesitated. Then, unable to stop himself, he said, 'I think perhaps this is how I should like to spend every Christmas.'

He held his breath.

Seconds passed. Caroline stared down at her plate, the fire crackling behind them, before she finally whispered, 'I should like that, too.'

He blinked, caught entirely unprepared by her admission. Yet he kept his expression calm, unwilling to startle the moment. Inside, however, joy welled like a spring beneath stone — quiet, powerful, and unstoppable. It was a step. A step towards everything he hoped for.

* * *

Do not encourage his attentions!

He deserved far better than herself,

but Caroline could not help grasping onto the possibility that, come next year, she might return to visit him. If William were still unwed then — as she most certainly would be — it would be heavenly to rejoin him in this festive fantasy. When she left this evening, she could carry the promise of their reunion like a charm in her reticule. When she awoke alone in her bed, and the old memories threatened to devour her, she could turn her thoughts to this one sweet hope — a future respite from her solitude.

When they finished eating, she offered him a second helping, which he accepted. Carrying their plates to the back room, she replenished his plate fondly. A large man like William clearly required far more sustenance than she. Chuckling to herself, she carefully arranged some choice cuts of chicken and placed a generous wedge of mince pie beside them. She hummed softly as she poured more tea, then returned to the parlour with the tray, setting it down with care.

Moving about the room, she straightened the cushions and stoked the fire in the hearth. She had grown accustomed to his home, and the thought of leaving it behind — to return to her silent rooms — was depressingly bleak.

'Do you have someone to look in on you in the morning?'

William stretched his neck, rubbing one shoulder. 'One of my apprentices will come by. I am hoping Dr. Hadley will give me permission to walk when he visits. The swelling has gone down quite a bit. I hope a second look will reveal that the sprain was not as bad as we first thought.'

Caroline wandered over, bending to peer at his ankle before gently probing it with her fingers. 'It certainly is better than when I first arrived.'

He nodded, then said hesitantly, 'If you sit with me, I can read to you.'

She took her seat beside him, and he reached for the book he had left on the table.

'What will you read me?' she asked,

settling in.

'It is Christmas,' he said, 'so I thought I would read verses from popular wassails.'

Throwing out an arm, he drew her close into the crook of it, resting his head lightly against hers. Reaching around her, he held the little book open and began to recite. The timbre of his voice stirred something gentle and unforeseen within her — a warmth that nestled beneath her ribs and refused to fade.

Huzza, Huzza, in our good town
The bread shall be white,
and the liquor be brown
So here my old fellow I drink to thee
And the very health of each other tree.
Well may ye blow, well may ye bear
Blossom and fruit both apple and pear.
So that every bough and every twig
May bend with a burden both fair and big
May ye bear us and yield us fruit such
a stors
That the bags and chambers and house
run o'er.

As he turned the page to find another, Caroline's eyes drifted shut. She surrendered to the crackle of the fire, the steady beat of his heart beneath her cheek, and the warmth of his voice washing over her like a balm.

This is what true happiness must feel like.

Soon, it would end. But until then, she would hold tightly to the promise of returning. Of spending next Christmas with him once more. The season could not come soon enough when she returned to the silence of her everyday life.

* * *

After reading for some time, William finished and reluctantly shut the book.

Caroline slowly opened her eyes and sat up, forcing him to relinquish his embrace. 'I suppose I must replace your poultice, provide you with some supplies, and then head home.' Her usually cheerful voice held a sorrowful intonation as she rubbed her eyes.

William licked his lips, wishing he could prolong their time together. 'Must you leave so soon?'

'I am not certain when my landlady will return, and I should be there when she arrives to avoid questions about where I have been.'

His throat thickened with emotion as she stood and moved away. Their time was ending, and the only promise he had secured was that she might return a year from now.

The intelligence that had built his business deserted him in the face of desperation to keep her with him — even a minute longer.

'What if I were to court you? Would that be acceptable?'

Caroline's expression crumpled. Had she been upset about leaving all along, if her emotions were this near the surface?

'Please trust me when I say you do not wish to pursue me. I am not worthy, William.'

He rubbed a hand over his chin,

searching for words. 'I believe you are.'

She shook her head. 'But I am not. You do not know what I have done.'

William's interest sharpened. Her secret — was it a matter of guilt? Perhaps if he could coax it from her, he might help her see what he had learned the night before: that blessings and burdens could exist together. She had saved him from the darkness. Could he not do the same for her?

'Please, come and sit with me?'

She returned to his side, sitting heavily. 'If I could, I would stay, William.'

'Then tell me — why do you feel you are unworthy of my attention? Perhaps, once it is spoken aloud, it will no longer seem so insurmountable.'

Her hands came together in agitation. 'If I tell you what I did, I shall lose your regard — and I do not want that.'

He brought his hand over hers in quiet comfort. 'Please, sunshine. There is nothing you could say to change my mind about you.'

Caroline's shoulders shook as she

swallowed a sob. 'It was unforgivable.'

'Nothing is unforgivable, if one seeks to make amends.'

'There is no way to fix what I have done.'

William tugged on his beard, his thoughts turning. 'Regardless, it cannot alter how I feel about the woman who cared for me on Christmas Eve.'

Her head lifted, her eyes locking with his. The torment in them struck him hard, but he met it with unwavering calm, lifting his hand to tuck a lock of hair behind her ear.

She was so achingly beautiful. He had to be strong — if he wanted her to be free of the past, she needed to see herself through his eyes.

'When I was thirteen, my grandmother died. She was my only living relation.'

William nodded, his chest tightening. She had been only a little older than he was when his own parents died — only he had Uncle Albert. She had had no one.

'Mrs. Harris had known my grandmother and promised me a position when the time came. So I went to work at Baydon Hall, where she was the housekeeper.' She paused, so William stroked her cheek to encourage her.

'Miss Annabel was the daughter of a baron. She was younger than I but took me under her wing. She taught me to read, helped with sums. When she saw how skilled I was with a needle, she gave me fabrics. She even convinced Mrs. Harris to apprentice me. We spoke of me opening a dress shop one day — and she vowed to invest her pin money in it when she married.' Caroline's voice broke.

William put an arm around her, drawing her gently in. 'What did you do?'

Caroline buried her face in his shoulder. 'The Earl of Saunton began courting Miss Annabel when she turned nineteen. Soon they were betrothed. He visited often and I — I frequently met him in secret.'

William held her tightly as she sobbed, stroking her back. 'You blame yourself for behaving improperly?'

'Nay, William — for betraying my friend. Annabel gave me everything, and I deceived her.'

William tried to imagine himself in her place. If he had stolen Nellie from Charles . . . The guilt would have consumed him. He understood.

'What happened?'

'She caught us kissing in the stables.'

Gad!

'She gave me a reference. She had Mrs. Harris place me with a doctor's household.'

That was remarkably generous. Perhaps Caroline had not overstated their bond.

'And did she marry the Earl of Saunton?'

Caroline sniffled. 'Nay. She married the Duke of Halmesbury.'

William blinked. 'The duke? From Wiltshire?'

'Yes. You know him?'

'Of course. His estate is not two hours from here. But Caroline — did Miss Annab — Her Grace — refuse your apology?'

Caroline pressed her face harder against him. 'I never apologised.'

'Why not?'

'She sent me away. There was no chance to say anything.'

'Have you tried since?'

'No . . . but she would not want to see me.'

He saw it then — how grief and shame had closed her world. Just as he had locked himself away from life after Charles's death.

'Why does this prevent you from accepting my courtship?'

'I vowed not to form any close connections. I cannot be trusted. Not with friendship. Not with affection. Certainly not as a wife.'

William frowned. 'When did this happen?'

'Two years ago.'

'And have you done anything similar since?'

'No.'

'Then I stand by what I said. You made

a single mistake. One you clearly regret. You have not repeated it. That speaks of strength, Caroline, not weakness.' He looked at her squarely. 'I remain committed to my desire to court you.'

She stared up at him. 'My character does not repulse you?'

'I am not repulsed. We all err. What matters is what we do after.'

How could she not see the truth? She had helped Annie Greer. She had tended William without question. And with her words, she had dragged him out of the shadows. If she would let him, he could do the same for her.

'I wish to court you, sunshine.'

He could see she was thinking about it, his mouth growing dry with nervous anticipation. Now that she had confessed the truth and received his heartfelt reassurance, would she relent on her vow? Seconds stretched into aching minutes as her emotions flickered across her face, and William bit his lip to remain silent, not daring to interrupt her deliberation.

'I cannot.'

Her words cracked the silence like a whip, a deafening blow. William's hand rose to his chest, half-expecting to find it cracked open, bleeding his life's essence. He had awoken from years of living half-dead, only to fall violently in love over the span of mere hours — only to have his esteem rejected.

Surely his heart had physically broken?

He struggled for words. His hand lifted to rub at his beard, quelling the urge to tear at his hair in helpless desolation.

And yet — he feared he was being selfish.

He had found a lifeline to happiness and clung to it with both hands, hauling himself back to shore with all his strength. But what of Caroline? What of her needs? She was in anguish over what she had done to her former mistress, and he knew well the cruelty of guilt. How it could cleave through the soul, leaving one broken and bleeding. How it could convince you there was nothing left to live for — not a single blessing to grasp.

He did not want to let go.

But that was precisely why he must.

With great reluctance, William accepted what she needed. And at present, it was not him. If there were ever to be a future together, he must put her first — even if it meant letting her go.

It was the hardest thing he had ever done, save for watching Charles die. But he did it anyway. Because Caroline needed him to. And because love demanded it.

One day, perhaps, they would find their way back to each other.

But not today.

He reclined against the cushions, forcing himself to remain still. 'I . . . understand.'

Caroline looked as if he had struck her. She blinked several times before clearing her throat and rising to her feet. 'All right, then. I am . . . glad you understand.'

William gave a single nod, closing his eyes so he would not be tempted to reach for her. She hesitated, lingering as though expecting him to object.

He did not.

He had pushed too far already. Now he must retreat — if only to preserve what hope might remain.

'I shall collect my things and go home.'

Another pause. Another silence. Then: 'Goodbye . . . William.'

His throat worked, but he said nothing. Only nodded again — tight, controlled.

Letting her walk away was agony.

But it was the only way forward.

9

The Truth

Saint Stephen's Day (The Second Day of Christmas)

Caroline was bent over the walking dress when she heard Annie approaching the shop. It lifted her flagging spirits to know she would have company that day, so she paused and tilted her head to listen to the carol.

The twelfth day of Christmas,
My true love sent to me,
Twelve lords a leaping,
Eleven ladies dancing,
Ten pipers piping,
Nine drummers drumming,
Eight maids a milking . . .

The back door opened, and the singing was no longer muffled as Annie drew a deep breath to complete the lengthy verse in her sweet, youthful voice. Her clear tones filled the room, rising and falling with the cadence of the carol, lending a brightness to the room. Caroline paused in her stitching, allowing herself the luxury of simply listening.

Seven swans a swimming,
Six geese a laying,
Five gold rings,
Four colly birds,
Three French hens,
Two turtle doves, and
A partridge in a pear tree.

Annie walked over to the worktable where Caroline was seated and finished her song with a flourish, clearly proud of herself for recalling all the lines correctly.

'Happy St Stephen's Day, Mrs. Brown!'

Caroline forced a cheery smile onto her tired face. She had been miserable since leaving the blacksmith's home the day before and had not slept a wink all night. Considering how their time together had ended, she did not know what to make of their connection.

Did they even have one, after she had rejected his suit?

'Happy St Stephen's Day, Annie!'

The child gave a little curtsey, then asked a question that must have been troubling her. 'What is a colly bird, Mrs. Brown?'

''Colly' means black, like coal.'

'Oh. So the fourth day is about blackbirds?'

'It would seem so. The song is originally French, so there may be errors in translation, but I think blackbirds is correct.'

'And why do you think so many days are about birds, but not the fifth day?'

Caroline shrugged. 'Some say the gold rings are gold ring-necked pheasants. I have never seen one myself, but they are supposed to be quite colourful.'

Annie nodded, her attention already drifting to a new subject, as children often did.

'We had a wonderful Christmas feast.

Mr. Andrews joined us after closing his shop, and Mum made you some black butter.' Annie placed a little pot on the table. Caroline picked it up and opened the lid to inhale the fruit paste's distinctive scent with pleasure.

'Tell your mum thank you. I shall buy some fresh bread to eat it with!'

Annie nodded and tied on her apron. 'I think Mr. Andrews is sweet on Mum. He invited us to go wassailing on Twelfth Night.'

Caroline gritted her teeth in exasperation. Perfect. Mrs. Greer would have a new husband before long, while Caroline would remain alone forever — while a perfectly good man lay, rejected, on his settee down the street. And not just any man — William.

She missed him something fierce.

Have I made the right decision?

Realising she had not responded, she forced a cheery tone and asked the important question. 'How do you feel about that?'

Annie paused to consider, her little

face pensive. 'I think Mr. Andrews is a jolly man. And he makes excellent food, so I suppose it would be all right if he courts Mum.'

Caroline chuckled — for the first time all day. 'Excellent food will always be acceptable.'

Annie grinned back. 'I shall fetch your bread for you, if you like. Mr. Andrews might give me a Sally Lunn bun if I visit his shop.'

'Then I have no choice. I shall have to allow you to run the errand for me. Tell Mr. Andrews to put it on my account.'

'Shall I sweep the front?'

'Yes. I want to work on my walking dress, and I expect little custom today. When you finish sweeping, you can come and sit with me and I'll show you what I'm doing.'

The girl nodded and disappeared through the workroom door — only to race back a moment later, a worried expression on her face.

'Mrs. Brown! Some of the Christmas boughs are missing!'

A nervous twist tightened in Caroline's stomach. She had forgotten the boughs. After the abrupt end to her day with William, she had left them behind without a second thought.

'I . . . gave them to someone who needed them more than I.' She needed to distract Annie quickly. 'Did you complete the handkerchief you were sewing?'

The girl looked down, her expression guilty. 'No . . . I was too busy helping Mum make the Christmas boughs.'

'You can join me when you are done sweeping and finish it then.'

Annie brightened. It was a shameful manipulation on Caroline's part — an effort to change the subject — but it would not do to have anyone asking questions about how she had spent Christmas.

* * *

William had convinced Dr. Hadley that he was recovered enough to be back on his feet. The doctor had bound his ankle, cautioning him to be careful and not to overexert himself, but had concurred that the sprain was not as severe as it had first appeared on Christmas Eve.

He had then requested the use of the doctor's carriage, a favour which Dr. Hadley had also granted, though they had haggled for some time. The physician had been reluctant to charge him for the loan, while William had insisted upon paying a rental fee. Eventually, they had struck a mutually agreeable bargain, and the doctor departed to see the carriage made ready.

St Stephen's Day was the perfect occasion to call upon a lady of quality. It was a day of charitable observance, when the doors of respectable households opened to the community. William intended to take full advantage of the festive traditions to aid Caroline.

He was committed to her healing, as she had been committed to his. She had comforted him in his darkest hour, untethered him from his torment over

Hougoumont, and reminded him how to breathe again. He could not let her suffer in silence. She deserved peace. She deserved joy.

Eventually, he hoped she would forgive his clumsy intrusion into her privacy — if he succeeded in his purpose.

William washed with haste but took great care with his attire. He donned a pristine white shirt, followed by his finest stockings and best breeches — the pair reserved for Sundays and significant occasions. Then he polished his buckled shoes, grimacing at the thought of wearing them, but boots were impossible with a bound ankle. Besides, the shoes were more elegant.

He tied his cravat with precision, shrugged into his navy wool tailcoat, and retrieved his hat and walking cane from the stand.

He cast one last glance around the cottage, suddenly aware of how different it looked with hope stirring in his chest. It was imperative that he be well received where he was going. As much as he disliked formal dress, he would do whatever it took to restore Caroline's spirits.

* * *

Caroline worked on the walking dress she had spent so many months perfecting, but it brought no solace. Her magical holiday interlude was over. Nothing remained but a memory to hold dear. She feared she had greatly disappointed the blacksmith — and the more she thought on it, the less sense it made to have walked away.

But then, he had so abruptly changed his mind and allowed her to go. Perhaps he had reflected on her faults and lost interest in pursuing her further.

Annie entered from sweeping the front. Fetching her needles and some thread, she came to take a seat beside Caroline at the worktable.

'You do not appear to be in good spirits, Mrs. Brown?'

'I am sad that Christmas is over,' she

offered by way of explanation.

Annie twisted her mouth in perplexity. 'Christmastide is not over. It only ends on Twelfth Night. There are many celebrations ahead.'

Caroline's hand froze mid-stitch, struck by the simplicity of the child's logic. Children often cut through the fog of emotion with a single, unadorned truth. Why was she here, pining, when William had accepted her, flaws and all, and offered a future she had never dared to imagine?

Had fear driven her decision? Was it still driving her now?

It was not too late. Perhaps she could take a chance on herself. After all, punishing herself indefinitely might not be the noblest course — not when a man as generous and steadfast as William wished to share his life with her.

But if she were to allow his courtship, she would need to confess how she had come to own her shop. Her stomach twisted at the thought. How had she omitted that detail when laying bare her past? Could she bring herself to tell him that Lord Saunton had lent her the funds as an act of reparation? Would William view it as a business arrangement — or see her as a kept woman?

Why not visit him and see where the conversation takes you?

She dithered, staring down at her needlework. 'I have an errand to run. Can you mind the shop for an hour, or should I close it?'

Annie raised her eyebrows in surprise but asked no questions. 'I can mind the shop.'

Caroline set aside her work, hung the gown reverently in its place of honour, and donned the cloak William had once teased her about. If he proved understanding, perhaps she would wear this very gown on her wedding day.

She exited from the back and hurried down the alleyway, reaching the block where William's cottage stood — only to find the streets were too crowded. She could not approach his home unseen. If Mrs. Heeley had returned from Bath,

Caroline would be spotted for certain.

Loitering in hesitation, she realised she had lingered too long. Someone would soon take notice. She turned up the cross street to re-enter Market Street, striving for a solution.

Perhaps the smithy. He had hoped Dr. Hadley would clear him for work. He might be there now.

She headed towards the billowing chimneys, drawing her cloak tight as the wind sliced through her sleeves. Perhaps William was right about the garment's shortcomings. She could make a warmer one for days such as this — and keep this pretty, impractical thing for milder weather.

As she neared the smithy, it was clear the forge was in full operation. Shutters stood wide to release the heat, and the cacophony of hammers rang out over the clanging of metal.

She entered through the customer door, stopping at the counter that divided the waiting area from the work floor. Though it was her first visit to the smithy, the operation spoke of precision and prosperity. Three forges blazed with fire, giant bellows suspended behind them. Men used tongs to manipulate glowing iron, heating it to a cherry red.

Apprentices swept coal shards, stoked the flames, and worked bellows with strong arms and quick coordination. Several journeymen laboured at anvils, hammering with unrelenting rhythm. The sound was deafening. Caroline raised her fingers to her ears.

On the counter lay catalogues of locks and tools. The wall behind displayed a selection of wares — everything neatly organised, efficient, professional. A section dedicated to steel held especially fine work, likely the smithy's highest earners. A boy of about fifteen spotted her and hurried over, wiping his hands on a leather apron. She removed her fingers from her ears.

'Can I help you, ma'am?'

'I was looking for Mr. Jackson. Is he here today?'

'No, ma'am. He took the day to travel

to Bath. Said something about visiting someone for St Stephen's Day.'

A man near the forge turned and guffawed. 'More like gone a-courting, dressed in his Sunday finest!'

Laughter rippled across the smithy, men making jest of the blacksmith being sweet on someone in Bath.

Caroline stood motionless. *Gone to Bath? Visiting another woman?*

All she could think of was how unbearably inconvenient it was to realise she loved William at the precise moment she learned she might have lost him. Her heart squeezed painfully. Fighting tears, she willed her voice to remain steady.

'I was speaking with him about . . . repairing a lock. I will return tomorrow.'

She swept out before the apprentice could respond. Turning back onto Market Street, she passed her shop without pause. Her feet carried her without instruction, her thoughts in chaos. She had lost her chance. He had offered her everything — his name, his loyalty, his heart — and she had refused him. And now? Gone to Bath, they said. Courting another, perhaps.

The wind whipped past the shopfronts, cold and punishing. She wrapped her arms around her middle, bracing against the ache in her chest. Perhaps the men had misunderstood. William had not struck her as fickle. But now she had no way of knowing when he might return — or whether she would still be in his heart when he did.

She had been foolish to let herself believe in connection. Foolish to break the vow that had preserved her peace. Connections could be lost. And when they were, one was left only with the ashes of regret.

Work is the answer.

10

The Reconciliation

The Fifth Day of Christmas

She had not caught a glimpse of the blacksmith in several days, but there he was, across the street, entering the post office. If she hurried out there, she could catch him on his way out and determine once and for all if she had lost her opportunity.

Over the past three days, since visiting the smithy and learning he was gone to Bath, Caroline had worked under a shroud of turmoil. One moment she was committed to working, the next she was wondering, what if?

What if William was not courting another woman?

What if this was a misunderstanding, and his offer to wed was still valid?

What if they could form a wonderful union, two successful proprietors united in a partnership? Assist each other in realising their respective dreams?

For the first time in days, she might have an opportunity to find out where matters stood.

'I think perhaps I would like to see the blue silk again.'

'Miss Jolie, Lady Jolie, would you mind if my apprentice assisted you for just a moment? I see someone I must converse with, but I will be right back.'

The young woman and her mother nodded, still fingering the fabrics they were inspecting. Caroline brought out the silk they had requested while calling for Annie, keeping a nervous eye out for William to ensure she did not miss him, before hurrying out the front door.

Crossing the street, she stopped outside the post office, fidgeting with her gown while she tried to decide if she should follow him in. Leaving her shop without a cloak had been ill-advised — she was quickly growing cold in the winter air, but if she entered, they could hardly speak of anything meaningful.

Just as she raised her hand to enter, she saw William approaching from the other side of the door and stepped back to allow him to exit. He caught sight of her through the glass panes and appeared to hesitate for a moment, as if he were preparing himself before he opened the door and strode out.

'Mrs. Brown, season's greetings.' His words were polite, but the intonation was flat, as if he were parroting appropriate behaviour.

Caroline gave a slight curtsey in greeting. 'Mr. Jackson, I . . . wanted to discuss that lock.' She glanced restlessly towards the two women passing behind him. William stared over her shoulder, refusing to meet her eyes.

Realising William would not look at her, Caroline's heart sank. So it was true. William had moved on after her rejection. He had found someone who would appreciate him — something she had failed to do.

'However, it is not urgent. I shall visit you at the smithy when I have time.' She stepped back, her hopes and what-ifs finally dashed to pieces like the waves hitting rocks in the seascape over his mantel. Which she would never see again — not this Christmas or the next.

William put out a hand as if to stay her. 'Mrs. Brown, I — ' He stopped, his eyes focused on a point over her shoulder. It was clear he had been about to say something, but now he stood taciturn, even unnerved. Behind her, she could hear the rumble of wheels. ' — I must go!'

With that, he abruptly turned to storm down the street. Caroline was left to watch his retreating form until she was distracted by how loud the approaching vehicle was.

Frowning, she turned around to see what had caught his attention and discovered that a large, ornate carriage, pulled by a perfectly matched set of four chestnut geldings, was approaching. Liveried servants could be seen in blue with gold brocade. Someone important must be visiting Chatternwell.

Realising she had left Miss Jolie and her mother alone with Annie and a promise to return, Caroline quickly crossed the street to re-enter her shop. The warmth was a relief, even if it could not warm her frozen heart.

'Miss Jolie, my apologies. I . . . had a lock that needed repair, and Mr. Jackson happened to be passing by.'

'It is no trouble, Mrs. Brown. I shall have the gown made with the Saxon blue silk, if you could?'

Caroline blinked in surprise. It was one of her most expensive fabrics, so the order would include substantial profit. It appeared her business would continue to thrive while inside she floundered. She nodded, pulling out her order book to write down the details.

Shortly, the two women exited the shop, chattering about a visit to the haberdashery next door. That was when Caroline realised that the elegant carriage she had seen approaching earlier had stopped in front of her shop, and a footman stood at attention.

Lady Jolie and Miss Jolie paused, peering curiously at the carriage. It was the finest Caroline had ever seen, with an intricate coat of arms on the door, luxurious drapery in the windows, and a gilded finial at the crest of the slanting roof.

The footman continued to stand at attention, paying no mind to the two women gawking at him. Eventually, they moved off, casting inquisitive glances over their shoulders as they walked away.

Caroline was transfixed, staring at the carriage. As soon as the two women disappeared from sight, the footman sprang into action, as if he had been awaiting their departure. He reached up to open the carriage door, then fixed the steps in place before stepping aside.

Highly polished black riding boots came into view on the top step, followed by buckskins draped over powerful legs, and then a man descended. A very large Viking of a man, several inches over six feet, with blond hair and an elegant blue tailcoat.

Caroline blinked rapidly, trying to place him, before her mouth fell open. It was the Duke of Halmesbury!

The earl had briefly introduced them back in August when she had visited Lord Saunton at Chatternwell House to sign her loan documents.

The duke turned and held up a hand to assist a woman to descend from the dim interior. All Caroline could make out was the expensive hem of a burgundy carriage dress, the duke blocking most of her view, but blood began to pound loudly in her ears.

There could only be one woman who would accompany the duke in the ducal carriage — Caroline was about to meet her past.

'Annie!' The girl came running from the back, clearly alarmed at the sharpness of her employer's voice.

'Yes, Mrs. Brown?'

Caroline drew a breath to modulate her tone. 'Please run over to Mr. Andrews and purchase some pies for us.'

Annie's brown eyes brightened in

anticipation. A visit to Mr. Andrews was certain to earn her a sticky bun. 'Yes, Mrs. Brown.'

As the child turned away, Caroline called out, 'And, Annie, take your time. I need to meet with this customer in private.'

Annie nodded vigorously, more than happy to have some time to herself as she skipped to the back. Fortunately, Mrs. Jones and her daughter were not working today, so Caroline had the shop to herself. And her unexpected guest.

Outside, the duke stepped aside to reveal his wife. Miss Annabel, chestnut hair neatly coiffed and brandy eyes shining, sought her out through the windowpanes. Caroline flushed as their gazes met, licking her lips and wiping her damp palms over her skirts to still their trembling while Her Grace approached the door.

The footman opened it, stepping back to allow the duchess entry and then shutting the door behind her. This was to be a private audience.

Caroline and Her Grace stared at each other across the shop for several seconds before Caroline recalled her place and sank into a deep curtsey. 'Miss Anna— Your Grace.'

The young woman laughed out loud. 'No matter how long I am married to the duke, I never grow accustomed to how old acquaintances behave because of my increased station as his wife. It is' — the duchess tilted her head as if seeking the right word — 'disconcerting.'

'My apologies, Your Grace.'

The duchess walked over to where Caroline was awkwardly posed in the curtsey, uncertain if she was to rise in these circumstances. 'I have come to visit an old friend, so perhaps you should rise and we can converse freely.'

Caroline choked as she returned to a standing position and rubbed at her dry throat. When she regained the ability to speak, she sputtered, 'Old friend?'

Her Grace tilted her head again, contemplating her with a sad expression. 'Were we not friends?'

Her throat muscles worked, and eventually, Caroline croaked her response. 'Until I ruined it.'

'Hmm.'

'What are you doing here?' Caroline clapped a hand over her mouth at the shrill demand. 'Your Grace,' she added in an attempt to soften her high-strung tone.

'I received a visit from a Mr. Jackson on Saint Stephen's Day. He told me you were in dire need of an audience with me. He seemed to think that I was a woman of noble character who would be magnanimous if I were to understand your troubles.'

Caroline's eyes widened in horror. To do such a thing! Rage rose as a heavy feeling in her head, making her feel giddy from the force of it. The Sunday finest! He had not been to Bath to court a lass. He had been to the ducal estate to visit the duchess!

William was rude, insufferable, arrogant, invasive, and . . . and . . .

'Sweet? Loyal? Determined to secure

your happiness?' the duchess responded.

Caroline clapped a hand over her mouth again. Had she spoken the words out loud?

'You did. What struck me during his visit was that you must care deeply about this man if you shared your secret with him. I was very pleased to discover that a man of such quality had taken it upon himself to speak on your behalf, but grew concerned when he informed me that his offer to marry you had been declined because of our shared history. Which is why I agreed to visit you. I would have come earlier, but this is the first day of Christmastide that did not have specific obligations to attend to.'

Caroline nodded. Yesterday had been the Feast of the Holy Innocents, and the day before had been the Feast of Saint John the Evangelist. As her thoughts skittered about inanely, Caroline realised she was procrastinating due to shock. Ransacking her mind, she located her senses to finally say something that was . . . not deplorable. 'I have long wanted . . . to apologise for my actions.'

The duchess nodded, setting her rich red-brown curls to bouncing. 'This conversation is overdue.' She turned and walked away to inspect the interior before coming to a stop by the door and glancing about to take it all in at once. 'The shop is exactly as we imagined it as girls.'

'I thought of you often when I was preparing it for opening.'

Her Grace turned her head to gaze at her directly. 'I have thought of you often, too. I was very pleased when I heard that Lord Saunton had taken responsibility for you and was financing our plans in my stead.'

Caroline inhaled in surprise. 'You were? Why?'

'I never wished you ill. Your actions precluded us from continuing on together, and I will admit I was furious for a few weeks, but then my situation changed. What happened between us . . . it led me to the duke. If I had not caught you and Lord Saunton together, we would be unhappily married, but instead, I am married to a wonderful man whom I needed. Who needed me. Now we have a strong young boy we both adore.'

Caroline slumped as she listened to this declaration, tears stinging in threat. 'It is so comforting to hear I did not ruin your life!'

The duchess frowned. 'Ruined my life? No. Lord Saunton was the very worst of rakes until he met his wife. We would have had a disastrous marriage.'

Caroline swiped the tears from her lashes with a trembling hand. 'I am so happy for you . . . truly . . . but . . . hearing that . . . why do I still feel guilt? It has been two years, and the shame has not worn off.'

Her Grace said nothing, contemplating the question until she sighed heavily. 'Lord Saunton informed me he had to release the guilt. That it was not about what I thought of him, but what he thought of himself. He had to make reparations to the women he had wronged to reach a point where he could trust himself.'

'I do not understand.'

'It is not my place to forgive you. Forgiveness must come from within. None of us are free of mistakes, so you will have to find a way to come to terms with what you did.'

'I do not know how!' cried Caroline, feeling desperate to be so close to resolution yet still not finding what she was seeking.

The duchess walked forward, stopping before Caroline to take up her hands and stare into her eyes. Caroline was enthralled by the warm gold and brown striations, unable to look away.

'Why did you do it?'

'I was so lonely. No man had ever paid attention to me before, and Lord Saunton was . . . charming and solicitous.'

'Be that as it may, what was the cost to your self-respect?'

Caroline shook her head. 'Far beyond what I would be willing to pay if I were presented with similar circumstances in the future.'

'So you have considered your mistakes and learnt from them?'

'I have.'

'And now I have assured you there was no lasting damage, and it all worked out for the best.'

'Which is gratifying to hear.'

'Then what do we do to restore your faith in yourself?'

'I suppose . . . speaking with you is the first step. I was initially angry when you told me Mr. Jackson had manipulated this meeting, but now . . . I needed to see you. To express my regret.'

Miss Annabel nodded. 'When I heard how deeply concerned Mr. Jackson was for your happiness . . . He is a good man.'

Caroline bit her lip, thinking about what came next. What could she do to ease her guilt? She had taken pains not to repeat her past, and the duchess had said it had all turned out for the best — which was a balm to hear — but still . . . she needed to offer some token of her regret.

Nay! Not a token of my regret, but rather

a token of my esteem — to demonstrate how much I value our shared past!

Despite her actions to the contrary, Caroline had always valued her connection to Miss Annabel and Mrs. Harris. She needed to express her love and appreciation for all they had done to secure her current success — for leading her to her dreams. For teaching her strength.

But how?

'Could I do something for you? Perhaps . . . make you something?' Her hand flew over her mouth at once, mortified. 'I apologise. Of course, you are a duchess, and anything I create would be far too inferior!'

The duchess frowned, twin furrows appearing between her brows. 'Do not disparage yourself. I would be honoured to receive a gift from Chatternwell's preeminent modiste.'

Modiste!

Until that very moment, Caroline had thought of herself as an audacious maid who had reinvented herself as a dressmaker in a small town. Now she swelled with pride as she considered herself a fashionable modiste — offering one of her creations to a duchess of the realm. Her mind raced with possibilities. Her Grace had seen that potential in her as a girl and had come to verify her welfare. That revelation shifted Caroline's very sense of self.

'I could' — Caroline glanced around, frantically searching for an idea fit for a duchess — until her eyes landed on the door of the coach out on the road — 'present you with a very fine walking dress embroidered with the Halmesbury coat of arms!'

The duchess's eyes widened before lighting with delight. She turned to peer out the window at her husband. Silence reigned for several seconds before she turned back, lashes glistening with unshed tears. The duke, watching from his position outside, frowned in concern, straightening to peer pensively into the shop.

'That would be unique and highly

valued.'

Tears of joy sprang into Caroline's eyes, overcome by the dense emotion that filled the room. 'I have worked on such a dress for months. I shall personally embroider it. It can be ready for you by tomorrow.'

'We are spending the night at Chatternwell House, so I shall speak with the duke about delaying our return until tomorrow afternoon.'

Her Grace returned to the door. The footman sprang forward to open it. Out on the road, she conferred with her husband in hushed tones, then returned to the shop.

'His Grace agrees. Shall I try the dress on? The footman will bring you a cushion from the carriage with the coat of arms to use as a template.'

'Yes. Thank you . . . Miss Annabel.'

The duchess grinned at the use of her name from their youth. 'My pleasure . . . Caroline.'

Caroline led her into the back, where the gown hung. Gazing at it, she felt a twinge of regret. Only days ago, she had thought of marrying in it. But it would now serve a greater purpose — as the key to unlock a future unmarred by guilt or shame. A symbol of how far she had come, of her regrets, and a new beginning more profound than the opening of her shop.

'It is exquisite,' proclaimed the noblewoman, fingering the fabric.

'The finest velvet I could find. I bought it from the docks in London, directly from the merchant who shipped it in.'

Caroline took it down. The duchess removed her carriage dress, revealing an ivory linen gown beneath. She raised her arms and slipped into the walking dress. Buttoning it up, she moved before the mirror, posing at various angles.

'What do you think of the colour? Do you think we suit — your dress and I?'

'You . . . are utterly beguiling in it. It is as if it was always intended for you.'

'And the coat of arms?'

'I shall embroider it with gilt floss on the back.'

'That will be striking against the Prussian blue. This is your finest work.'

Caroline examined the garment, draping it as she noted what alterations were needed. 'It is, and it is only fitting that I made it for you. I shall let the cuffs out for your longer arms and re-hem it because you are a little taller, but those appear to be the only adjustments required. If I work through the night, it shall be ready by early afternoon.'

'Perfect. That will allow us time to return to Avonmead before sunset.'

Caroline helped Her Grace remove the dress, and they returned to the front of the shop.

'Thank you for taking such trouble to come and see me, Your Grace.'

'It sets my mind at ease to know you are succeeding. You have put a great deal of work into this.' Impulsively, the duchess embraced her. 'I am so happy you found someone who appreciates you. Take care of him — and do not be too angry with him for interfering.'

Caroline nodded, but her thoughts

were already elsewhere — on the dress. William could wait. For now.

She returned to the back as Annie entered from her errand, but Caroline paid her no mind, muttering about a deadline. All she could think about was how she wanted every ounce of respect and love she felt for Miss Annabel to be reflected in her work. The gratitude for all those years of encouragement. The care she had received when she was lost and alone. The regret —

Nay. I refuse to linger on the mistake.

Taking the gown to the window-lit table, she began to work. Annie brought tea and set it on the table, but Caroline did not notice. She worked until her eyes were dried-out husks, and her lids would no longer glide smoothly. She moistened them with silver water and continued until her fingers bled from accumulated pinpricks. Dabbing them to avoid staining the cloth, she laboured on.

This was about restoring her self-worth — presenting a gift woven with the threads of her very soul. By remembering the good times, the wonderful moments shared with her truest friend, she found strength to keep going.

When the embroidery did not satisfy her, she unpicked the stitches and began again.

This would be perfection — worthy not just of a duchess, but of her oldest, most beloved friend. And so, as the minutes turned to hours, Caroline worked.

To her surprise, the more she toiled — snatching only brief naps — the better she felt. The black guilt that haunted her, the shadows of self-doubt, melted away.

Finally, as dawn broke over the hills of Chatternwell, she lifted her head. Laying the gown aside, she folded her arms on the table and, utterly spent, fell into a deep, dreamless sleep.

11

The Gift

The Sixth Day of Christmas

William leaned over his anvil, sweat dripping from his chin as he panted from the exertion of his work. It was early. Too early for any of his men to have arrived at the smithy, but he had not been able to sleep. At last, he had surrendered to restlessness and risen from his bed.

The lock was almost complete.

If only he knew what was happening with his sunshine. He had been keeping his distance, not trusting himself to be near her. His longing to be with her was overpowering, but he had to give her time.

He had been both elated and apprehensive to observe the ducal carriage arriving on Market Street. The duchess had kept her word and visited Caroline. But had he been right to intervene between the two childhood friends?

And if it healed her soul, yet he lost her for ever because of his autocratic meddling, would it be worthwhile to know he had helped her reclaim her self-respect?

Raising a hand, he combed it through his damp hair and considered the possibility that they might never be man and wife. Could he live with that, if it meant she was happier? If he had succeeded in bringing her the peace she so sorely needed, even if she never forgave him for what he had done?

Since that night with Caroline, his nightmares had not returned. Now his dreams were haunted by something far worse.

When he fell asleep, he dreamed of her.

Like sunshine breaking through the bleak clouds of winter, his joy knew no bounds at being reunited with her — even if only in slumber. To touch her hand. To hear her voice. To feel the comfort of her presence.

But inevitably, he would awaken to

find himself alone in the dark.

Caroline had shown him how to live again, and he did not wish to return to the solitary existence that had consumed him since the war. He wanted to live. To feel. To experience life — with her. To witness her radiant generosity when they brought their future children into the world.

To him, she was the very embodiment of the holiday season, and he wanted her by his side every day from here on forward for the rest of his life. He wished he could walk out of the smithy and just go find her. Talk to her right now. But he was determined to allow her an opportunity to lay her past to rest and heal. His impatience to seek her out did not signify.

What had happened during the duchess's visit? Had Caroline found the peace she so desperately needed? Or did she hate him for his bungling interference?

* * *

Her Grace was not coming.

Caroline had waited all day for her return. Long shadows stretched across the street outside, signalling the approach of evening. The ducal carriage had not appeared.

She traced a fingertip over the delicate embroidery. She had unpicked the stitches and redone them several times. Absolute perfection had been required, and she had worked the Halmesbury coat of arms until her fingers ached with exhaustion.

It was all for nought.

She sighed heavily.

Was it a sign?

While she had laboured over the gown, she had swung between certainty and doubt. Should she seek William out? The duchess's failure to return suggested that Caroline had not earned her forgiveness in any genuine sense. She could only be grateful that the noblewoman had come at all.

'Mrs. Brown, would you like me to make you some tea?'

Annie's expression betrayed her concern. The girl had hovered nearby for some time, clearly worried by her employer's sombre mood. Though Caroline had attempted to maintain a cheerful countenance, her disappointment must have shown.

'That would be lovely, Annie.'

Caroline smoothed the gown and folded it gently into layers of silver paper, wondering what to do with it. Her own desire to wear it had long since vanished. In her heart, it already belonged to Her Grace. Perhaps she ought to have it delivered to Avonmead and close this chapter of her life.

Packing it carefully into a box, she carried it to the back and placed it on the highest shelf. Then she joined Annie near the fireplace for tea.

Just as she picked up the cup and saucer, the front door opened and closed.

She rose at once, heart in her throat.

It was the duchess.

Caroline's spirits ascended so sharply she felt dizzy.

'Mrs. Brown! I do apologise for the delay. We had trouble with one of the carriage wheels, and the duke wished to ensure it was repaired before nightfall. It appears the effort was successful, but we shall have to fly home come first light to make it to Avonmead for our Old Year's Day celebrations.'

The ducal carriage was visible through the front window. The duke and coachman stood behind it, inspecting one of the large rear wheels.

'I feared you had changed your mind, Your Grace.'

The duchess shook her head. 'Never! My word is my bond.'

'I am so glad you are here.'

'As am I. Is the dress complete?'

Caroline's chest tightened with nervous anticipation. She had taken such care with the embroidery. Every stitch had been deliberate. 'I shall collect it from the back.'

She retrieved the box from the shelf, butterflies taking flight in her stomach. So many hours had gone into the gown. Every spare minute over the past months — and the final burst of effort overnight.

It is my best work. It will have to do.

She brought the box to the front and set it on the counter. Her Grace joined her, and Caroline opened the lid, peeling back the silver paper to reveal the gown.

The duchess gasped, both hands rising to her cheeks. 'Oh! It is beautiful. You are an artist, Caroline!'

Caroline exhaled harshly, not realising she had held her breath. 'Truly?'

'It is breathtaking. Heraldic. May I try it on?'

'Of course.'

She led the duchess into the back room.

Annie stood at the hearth, her mouth ajar and eyes wide as the noblewoman entered. She collected herself swiftly, dropping into a curtsey. 'Milady.'

Caroline realised Annie had not met the duchess the day before. 'Your Grace, may I present Miss Annie Greer?'

'Your Grace?' the girl echoed, blinking.

'Cor!'

The duchess grinned. 'It is a pleasure to meet you, Miss Greer. How do you enjoy working for Mrs. Brown?'

'I love working here . . . Your Grace.'

'She is a remarkable artist. You will learn much as her apprentice.'

Annie nodded, eyes bright with admiration.

Caroline assisted Her Grace with removing her carriage dress and then with donning the walking gown. Stepping back, she admired the final effect.

The duchess's chestnut hair shimmered in contrast to the Prussian blue velvet, and the golden embroidery of the coat of arms glowed with quiet splendour across the back.

Her Grace turned this way and that in the mirror, then returned to the front of the shop. The duke had entered during their absence. When he saw his wife, his grey eyes lit with appreciation.

'Is it not splendid, Duke?'

'It is,' he said, his smile fond, 'but it cannot rival the beauty of the wearer.'

The duchess laughed sweetly, brushing a hand over the front of the gown. 'I adore it, Mrs. Brown. It is truly unique. I shall wear it when we visit our tenants on New Year's Day. I believe it shall cause quite the stir at Avonmead.'

Caroline exhaled, the tightness in her chest dissolving as the past fell away and an unencumbered future took its place. 'I am so pleased to have done this for you.'

After assisting the duchess in removing the gown and wrapping it once more in silver paper, Caroline watched as the noble couple took their leave. She stepped outside to see them off in the fading light, waving as the carriage rolled down the lane.

Looking down, she saw Annie had come to stand beside her.

'Do you think I shall make a gown for a duchess one day?'

'Anything is possible if you work hard and practise.'

'The dress was very beautiful, Mrs. Brown.'

'Thank you.'

'Are you sad it is not to be yours, like you intended?'

'Not at all. I did not realise it at the time, but it was always destined for Her Grace. Everything is as it should be.'

Caroline accepted the truth of it.

Two years ago, she had lacked the means to make amends. In the time since, she had worked diligently to hone her skills — even when it seemed unlikely she would ever open a shop of her own. When the chance had finally come, in the form of Lord Saunton's apology and offer of restitution, she had seized it — not for vengeance, but to pursue the dream she had once believed lost.

And then, as the final step, she had offered her gratitude to Miss Annabel. The walking dress had been her means of proving her worth, but giving it away — surrendering it not in defeat, but as a gift — had felt right. Its value had grown not in being worn, but in being offered to the one who most deserved it.

It had been her redemption.

Her peace.

Of course, none of it would have come to pass without a certain blacksmith who had seen fit to meddle.

What was she to do about William?

* * *

William stood on the road outside the smithy, taking a break from the heat of the forges to savour the wintry chill against his skin.

As he lifted his face to the cold breeze, a familiar sight caught his eye. The ducal carriage was gliding along Market Street.

His brow lifted. The duchess had returned for a second visit?

It must be a promising sign.

He supposed — hoped — that meant the past had been laid to rest.

Yet he still struggled to reconcile with his own audacity. He had demanded an audience with the wife of a duke. Not just any duke, but the Duke of Halmesbury — one of the most esteemed peers in the realm. A man of consequence and unassailable dignity.

What had possessed him?

Love, he supposed. Or something that looked very like it.

He gazed after the elegant carriage as it passed, then turned his thoughts towards Caroline.

Should he attempt to visit her?

His eyes dropped to his current state — his shirt soaked with sweat from hours of toil, hands black with soot, breeches bearing evidence of his labour. Hardly a suitable sight for calling on a lady, let alone the most admirable woman he had ever met.

No. Not today.

Tomorrow.

He would rise early and take the time to look his best. He would dress with care and visit Caroline as a gentleman should. If her conversation with the duchess had gone well, perhaps she might allow him to court her.

Please, let her allow it.

He wanted that future with Caroline so much he could taste it.

* * *

Caroline paced restlessly in her rooms, her slippers whispering against the rug with each turn. She had considered, dismissed, and reconsidered a hundred times whether to show up unannounced. The house was silent; her landlady had retired to her chambers three hours prior and would, by now, be well asleep.

Still, Caroline could not find peace.

In the distance, the mantel clock in the sitting room struck twelve, its chimes echoing through the quiet like a summons. Midnight.

She paused, biting her fingernail. Was it utter madness to seek him out at this hour?

The streets would be deserted. William's home was only a few streets away. And she could not rest until she knew — truly knew — where matters stood between them.

Her mind made up in a sudden rush of resolve, she donned her cloak and raised the hood. If anyone happened to see her, they might not recognise her in the dim light. Though she doubted anyone would be about at such an hour.

Easing open the front door, she slipped outside and closed it softly behind her. The cold was immediate, cutting and sharp, but she ignored it. She walked briskly, skirts rustling as she turned into the narrow alley that would lead her to Market Street. To William.

She could have waited until morning, of course, but then she would be forced to speak with him at the smithy — where privacy was impossible, and she might lose her courage. No, it had to be now. It was still Christmastide. The holiday magic had not yet waned. There might yet be time for them to reach an understanding.

As she approached Mrs. Heeley's cottage, her heart leapt into her throat, but all was dark and still. The widow must have remained in Bath. Thank heavens.

At last, she reached the blacksmith's back door. Her breath caught. Would the lock still be broken? If it had been repaired, and William had retired, there would be no way to summon him. She would have to turn back, chilled and defeated, and spend another sleepless night in a restless torment of what-ifs.

Her gloved hand, trembling with cold and something far more fragile, reached for the handle.

* * *

William sat in his drawing room, the fire crackling softly in the hearth as he nursed a cooling cup of tea. Sleep had proven elusive, and though he had planned to visit Caroline in the morning, something within him resisted the delay. The sense that time was fleeting, that the fragile magic of Christmastide might slip away before an understanding was secured, pressed down upon him like a weight.

He leaned forward, elbows on his knees, staring into the flames, attempting to make sense of his restless heart. Then came the sound. The soft creak of the back door. He straightened, alert.

Footsteps.

His heart hammered in anticipation. Then, from the dimness beyond, a voice — gentle and haunting — began to hum. He froze, wondering if he had fallen asleep and was once again caught in the grip of a magical dream. He made to rise, but then the humming began, causing him to blink and lean back.

Apparently, he had fallen asleep without realising it and was dreaming of her once more. Was it to be like the dreams from Christmas Eve? A visitation in which she revealed some truth to him?

Should auld acquaintance be forgot,
and never brought to mind?
Should auld acquaintance be forgot,
and auld lang syne?

'And there's a hand, my trusty fiere!
and gie's a hand o' thine!
And we'll tak' a right gude-willie waught,
for auld lang syne.'

He frowned, uncertain of his conclusion. If this were a mere conjuring in his dream, Caroline would sing the English lyrics with which he was familiar — not the original Scottish lyrics, which he did not know.

The door swung open, and there she was. His sunshine.

She stood illuminated by firelight and moonlight alike, her green cloak dusted with frost at the hem, her cheeks pink with cold. Her hands were clasped before her, but her eyes — those luminous hazel eyes — shone with emotion.

'Caroline?'

'You should repair your back door,' she said with a small smile, her voice trembling only slightly. 'Since it is gone midnight, I believe I may wish you a happy Old Year's Day.'

He took a step forward, drinking her in with his eyes. 'Is it truly you?'

She nodded. 'I was thinking about what you did. Visiting Her Grace on Saint Stephen's Day . . . it was no small gesture. I thought perhaps you might like to hear what came of it.'

'I would. More than you can know.'

'I have nothing grand to offer in return,' she said, removing her cloak and laying it across a chair. Beneath it, she wore her night rail, modest and familiar. 'But there is one thing I could give you. If you still want it.'

He stilled. 'What is it?'

She met his gaze. 'Me.'

The firelight crackled, casting golden light upon her determined face. William was speechless.

'I must return home before dawn,' she continued. 'But . . . once the banns are read . . . if you still wish it . . . I would like to become your wife.'

The words took a moment to register. And when they did, his heart surged with joy so fierce it nearly brought him to his knees.

'You are accepting my proposal?'

'I am.'

He reached for her, pulling her into his arms, embracing her tightly. 'You have no notion what this means to me,' he whispered against her hair.

'I believe I might,' she murmured.

They stood before the hearth, wrapped in each other's arms, the world narrowed to this one precious moment.

She lifted her face to his. 'I would like to remain here for a little while. To talk. And to be held.'

'There is nothing I should like more.' He kissed her, slowly, reverently, sealing the promise of their shared future.

When they finally parted, her cheek resting over his heart, he said quietly, 'I shall have to make a display of courting you come morning if we are to wed soon.'

'Tomorrow — or rather, later today — I shall close my shop early for Old Year's Day if you wish to spend some time with me in the afternoon.'

'Aye, we shall put on a show for our neighbours.'

'And you can accompany me to church on New Year's Day.'

'Aye, I shall speak to the curate to arrange a shared pew.'

'It is settled then, blacksmith.'

'Aye, modiste.'

'William . . . I did not tell you how I raised the loan for my shop.'

He heard the hesitation in her voice and realised she had a little more to confess. But tonight was meant for savouring their future together, and the details of how she had arrived in his life no longer signified. That was the past — this was their present.

'It shall not alter my feelings. Let us enjoy the holiday, and we can settle everything once the banns are read.'

She was quiet for several moments, presumably thinking on what he had said. At last, she replied, 'You are a good man, William.'

Caroline said nothing more after that. Hugging her close, William listened to her breathing as she gradually fell asleep in his arms, a broad grin of sheer happiness fixed in place. He could scarcely comprehend how much his life had changed in mere days. Solitude and shadows belonged to the past. Sunshine

would light his way as he stepped into the future.

Every day, from this day on, would be Christmas — with Caroline by his side.

Epilogue
The News

July 1821

My Dearest Mrs. Jackson,

Mr. Thompson and I are returning to Chatternwell to meet with the earl's Master Builder and greatly anticipate meeting your esteemed husband. Would you consider joining us for dinner after Sunday service on the 22nd of July? If you are amenable, we could send our carriage to collect you and Mr. Jackson and convey you to Chatternwell House. I do hope you can join us!

Warmest regards,

Jane Thompson

* * *

Caroline was humming in the drawing room when William came downstairs. He could live a hundred years and never tire of hearing his sunshine's melodies. With a smile, he entered the room to find her seated at the table with a cup of tea. It was evident she had already broken her fast before he had come down.

Their new housekeeper, who was tidying up, greeted him as she passed by on her way to the kitchen. 'Good morning, Mr. Jackson.'

'Mrs. Marlowe.' He nodded in acknowledgment.

Crossing the room, William ducked slightly to avoid the low ceiling beams, then bent to press a quick kiss to Caroline's temple before taking his place at the table. A moment later, Mrs. Marlowe returned with a plate of eggs and ham and set it beforc him.

'Thank you.'

She inclined her head and left them to their privacy.

'Annie came by this morning,' Caroline said, 'to inform me that Mrs. Greer has accepted an offer of marriage from Mr. Andrews.'

'At last! Mrs. Greer is a good woman and certainly deserves an improvement in her circumstances.'

'I am very pleased. Once she marries, I believe she will be helping the baker in his shop. It has been rewarding to assist a member of our community in building a future, so perhaps I shall offer similar employment to another widow in need of work.'

William nodded. 'That would be excellent. And what of Annie?'

'I asked whether she might wish to apprentice with the baker instead. I told her I would be agreeable to releasing her from our arrangement if her interests had changed, but she said she enjoys making pretty things.'

'That was generous of you.'

'I thought it important to be sure. But she has learnt much these past months, and I was relieved to hear she still wishes to continue with me.'

'I am gratified to hear it, especially

in light of the upcoming changes to our lives.'

She looked up from her teacup, her eyes catching the morning light. 'Are you speaking of our meeting with the Thompsons after services?'

'I am. From all accounts, Mr. Thompson is an excellent architect, and I expect an interesting conversation. Perhaps he can apprise me of the latest developments in London.'

'And I cannot wait to hear what his wife has to say about fashion. She has a special interest in the subject.'

William grinned. 'Will you tell her our news?'

Caroline tilted her head in consideration before glancing down at her belly. 'Not yet. Not until we have visited your uncle and aunt. They ought to be the first to know. They are the only family we have, after all.'

William rubbed a hand over his beard, thoughtful. 'I believe it shall bring them joy. Their letter in response to our marriage was very warm. I can only hope this news will give them even greater happiness.'

'Of course it will.'

He gave her a soft smile. 'You look lovely.'

She glanced down. She was wearing her mulberry walking dress, the one he most admired. 'The fichu is delightful, is it not?'

William squinted at the lacy gauze that modestly shielded her. 'Not as delightful as the one who wears it.'

She groaned and dropped her forehead into her hand. 'I am very much looking forward to speaking with someone who truly appreciates fashion later today!'

He chuckled and reached for her hand, lifting it to press a kiss to her knuckles. 'I am and always shall be a blacksmith, my love.'

'That is more than apparent.' Her tone was scolding, but her hazel eyes glowed with affection as she smiled back at him.

* * *

William and Barclay — the architect had insisted conversation would be much easier if they dispensed with formalities — were engaged in a spirited discussion regarding the lock William had recently perfected.

'Would you mind if we left the table, my dear?' Barclay inquired of his wife.

Jane Thompson smiled and shook her head. 'The meal is mostly finished. Please, go ahead.'

William glanced at Caroline, clearly seeking her assent. She offered a small nod, and the two men rose, animated by their shared enthusiasm. Barclay Thompson, tall and lean with a sweep of dark hair and a beard not unlike her husband's, had expressed an interest in partnering with William to produce the lock in London through his business connections. He foresaw considerable potential for profits in such a venture.

'I must confess,' Jane said with a wry smile once the gentlemen had left the room, 'I could no longer listen to the relative merits of brass versus zinc in the inner mechanisms of a lock.'

'May I go read my book now?' Little Tatiana looked up from her plate, her silvery-blonde hair escaping her plait, and her deep blue eyes wide with hope. The child was already lovely and would grow into a true beauty in time.

'Of course, darling. Mrs. Jackson and I shall be here if you need anything.'

The girl grinned, clearly eager to escape the dull company of adults. Rising quickly, she made her exit in a flutter of skirts, leaving Caroline and Jane to pick at the last remnants of their meal.

'I wished to remark upon your fichu,' Jane said after a pause. 'The lace is quite delicate.'

Caroline touched the fine edging, smiling softly. 'It was a wedding gift. From the Duchess of Halmesbury.'

'Oh! You know the duchess? The duke is Barclay's cousin.'

Caroline inclined her head. 'I was once in service at Baydon Hall for the Baron of Filminster. Her Grace was simply Miss Annabel then.'

Jane's expression changed, her brow creasing with concern. 'I do not suppose the news has reached Chatternwell yet.'

Caroline stilled. 'What news?'

Jane hesitated, clearly uncertain. 'I am not sure I ought to be the one to tell you, but as you will hear it soon regardless, I thought you might wish to send Her Grace a letter.'

Anxiety fluttered in Caroline's chest. 'What has happened? Is Her Grace unwell?'

'No, not directly.' Jane bit her lip, her discomfort evident. 'We nearly postponed our journey here due to a family emergency in London. The earl assured us that we were not specifically needed and should proceed with our plans.'

Caroline's fingers curled around the edge of her napkin. 'What sort of emergency?'

Jane exhaled. 'I regret to inform you that the baron was murdered three nights ago. In his London townhouse.'

'What?' Caroline clapped a hand over her mouth, realising too late that she had cried out.

'I am sorry.'

'I barely spoke to the baron during my years at Baydon Hall, but . . . how is Lady Halmesbury?'

'She is taking it in stride, though very distressed by the allegations being levelled against her brother.'

'Master Brendan?' Caroline's voice was strangled. 'That is not possible. He is the most amiable of men! And what was the baron doing in Town? He never left Filminster.'

'He was in London for the King's coronation. I do not know what the outcome will be regarding the charges, as we left for Wiltshire on Friday. Lord Saunton and the duke have been speaking with the coroner. We are cutting our visit short by a few days to return to Town as swiftly as possible.'

'This is a nightmare.' Caroline's voice had dropped to a whisper. 'They must have the wrong man.'

'I hope so. I truly do. Mr. Ridley is one of the warmest gentlemen I have ever met. You ought to see him with Jasper — the duke's heir. He has a marvellous way with children.'

Caroline nodded numbly, the horror of it unfolding in her mind. 'He would not — could not — commit such a heinous act. This must be a dreadful misunderstanding.'

'That is our hope, too. Perhaps by the time we return to Town, the true perpetrator will have been identified.'

Caroline's hands had gone cold. 'I shall write Her Grace a letter of condolence this evening.'

'She will be grateful for it, I am sure. I do not believe she was particularly close to the baron, but her concern for her brother is grave. If he is arrested and convicted . . .' Jane shook her head, her dark curls bouncing with the motion. 'I cannot even bring myself to say it.'

'It is unthinkable,' Caroline murmured.

'If you wish, I can provide you access to the library after dinner, and I shall take the letter back with me to deliver by hand. We are returning on Tuesday, so it will reach her before the week's end.'

'That would be most kind.'

* * *

Later that night, Caroline slipped into bed beside William. Cuddling up to him, she wrapped a slim arm about his waist and stared pensively at the opposite wall.

'Do not be distressed, sunshine. The duchess has many connections to assist her in the matter, and the duke is very influential. If anyone can sort out this muddle, it will be him.'

She smiled tremulously. William, setting aside his concern for Caroline, leant down to kiss her temple.

'Her Grace is surrounded by many allies. You can only control what you do here in Chatternwell. You ought to find someone to take on Mrs. Greer's work — someone hardworking and deserving of our support.'

Caroline nodded, tilting her head to gaze up at him in the darkened room.

'You are a good man, William Jackson.'

'And you taught me to count my blessings, Caroline Jackson. You are my greatest blessing of all.'

'Until our babe comes along.'

He chuckled, drawing her close. 'Until our babe is here. Then I shall have all the riches in the world.'

'Are you and Barclay to go into business together?'

'I believe so. He was impressed with the design. With the sort of connections he holds, we are certain to find the right men to work with.'

'I am pleased. Perhaps with his help, you shall have more time for creating designs.'

'So long as I live here with you for the rest of my days, anything I do for income is a blessing.'

She smiled, her cheek nestled against him as she gradually drifted off in his arms. 'I love you, blacksmith.'

'And I you, sunshine.'

William held her close, thankful to Providence for the radiance now in his life — soon to be multiplied by the arrival of their first babe. Caroline's worry for the duchess stirred an ache in his heart, but the knowledge that he could comfort and support her in this time of need was a blessing he would always cherish.

They were a family now — just as he had dreamt all those months ago.

Afterword

When I first scribbled down the idea for this book, I had no notion of just how much research I was setting myself up for. While much is known about the peerage, diving into the world of trades and the working classes revealed a labyrinth of challenges — far beyond the limits of my previous Regency knowledge.

Thankfully, a weekend in Colonial Williamsburg helped bring to life many essential details about both American and British trades, particularly how day-to-day business was conducted during the period.

Just when I thought I was back on track, another curveball arrived. What I assumed would be easy research into the holiday season turned out to be far more complicated, with conflicting accounts that forced me to dig deeper and untangle the discrepancies to uncover the truth.

But what fun it has been to research

dress rooms, blacksmiths, and Regency Christmas traditions!

Holiday customs during the period varied widely depending on the region, but those I described in this story are among those practiced during the Regency era. There is conflicting information about the precise dates of the Christmastide calendar, but I am reasonably confident I have gotten it right. I relied on the 1869 edition of *The Book of Days* (Chambers), the Church of England's celebration calendar, and a variety of other sources — including the writings of Charles Dickens himself.

The lyrics to *The Twelve Days of Christmas* used in this novel are from a version printed in Newcastle on an anonymous broadside between 1784 and 1825.

The lyrics to *Auld Lang Syne* are Robert Burns's 1788 version, which many will recognize as the traditional version sung during Old Year's Night (now more commonly known as New Year's Eve).

To my knowledge, it did not snow on December 24, 1820, in the Bath district — though it may have. I was unable to locate specific records of the weather for that day, so I ensured not to write in conflict with any known reports.

During the Regency, those attending church generally rented space in a pew or stood during the service — which is why William needed to visit the curate on Old Year's Day to arrange to share a pew with Caroline.

The silver paper Caroline used to pack the walking dress resembled white tissue, but was brighter, more translucent, and sturdier than that with which we are familiar today.

Curious about Dr. Hadley's treatments for William's sprain and his grave concern regarding the injury? William Buchan addressed strains and their dangers in his 1790 book, *Domestic Medicine*.

> *Strains are often attended with worse consequences than broken bones. The reason is obvious; they are generally neglected. When a bone is broken, the patient is obliged to keep the member easy, because*

he cannot make use of it; but when a joint is only strained, the person, finding he can still make a shift to move it, is sorry to lose his time for so trifling an ailment. In this way he deceives himself, and converts into an incurable malady what might have been removed by only keeping the part easy for a few days.

The skirmish at Hougoumont Farm is based on eyewitness accounts from the day, and Corporal James Graham — mentioned in this story — was indeed selected by the Duke of Wellington as the bravest non-commissioned officer at the Battle of Waterloo.

We do hope that you have enjoyed reading this large print book.

Did you know that all of our titles are available for purchase?

We publish a wide range of high quality large print books including:
Romances, Mysteries, Classics
General Fiction
Non Fiction and Westerns

Special interest titles available in large print are:
The Little Oxford Dictionary
Music Book, Song Book
Hymn Book, Service Book

Also available from us courtesy of Oxford University Press:
Young Readers' Dictionary
(large print edition)
Young Readers' Thesaurus
(large print edition)

For further information or a free brochure, please contact us at:
Ulverscroft Large Print Books Ltd.,
The Green, Bradgate Road, Anstey,
Leicester, LE7 7FU, England.
Tel: (00 44) **0116 236 4325**
Fax: (00 44) **0116 234 0205**

Other titles in the
Linford Romance Library:

LOVE IN THE FALL

Jill Barry

Tour guide Cassie discovers a celebrity is joining the Canadian trip she's leading, but fears author Jake may be troublesome. She's proved wrong during a whale-watching trip, when he rescues a drowning boy. Cassie and Jake's blossoming love is aided by their friendly coach driver, but when a tourist attracts the attention of jewel thieves, the couple's quick thinking pinpoints the culprits. The pair want to continue their relationship in London, despite their demanding jobs. Will love triumph?

FORBIDDEN LOVE

Kate Finnemore

Saxon maiden Mildritha is betrothed to the thane of Wolfsburh, and with that betrothal comes protection and security for her mother and sisters. When she discovers an injured man in the forest and helps him, however, Mildritha discovers what real love is. But he is a Norseman, the enemy of her people – and anyway, she can never break her promise to the thane . . .

ISLAND DREAMS

Evelyn Orange

Cassie Melrose inherits her grandmother's house and Craft Centre on the remote Scottish island of Arasay. Initially planning a brief visit, she becomes entangled in the island's charm, its close-knit community, and lingering emotions from her past — including a renewed connection with Zander, her teenage love . . .

LOVE ME TENDER

John Darley

Millie and her daughter have moved to Manchester for a fresh start, and so that Tammy can attend the university. Working at the local supermarket, Millie meets Dave, and they start a relationship. Tammy has become interested in finding her biological father, but Millie panics and deliberately gives her the wrong name to trace as she still feels embarrassed around the circumstances of her daughter's birth. However, Dave thinks that Tammy should be told the truth . . .

THE GIRL IN GREEN

Wendy Janes

When Beth's mother gifts her a beautiful watercolour of her much-missed grandmother as a little girl, she's intrigued to find out the identity of the artist. Beth starts by making an enquiry at a local art gallery, and is delighted when part-time art lecturer and gallery assistant, Edward, is eager to help in her quest.

Their search takes them on a journey of discovery. Can Edward help Beth unlock the mystery of the portrait . . . and her own heart?